By Joya Ryan

Yours Tonight
Yours Forever
Yours Completely

Yours Completely

JOYA RYAN

MIX
Paper from
responsible sources
FSC® C104740

Piatkus
An imprint of
Little, Brown Book Group
Carmelite House
50 Victoria Embankment
London EC4Y 0DZ

An Hachette UK company
www.hachette.co.uk

www.piatkus.co.uk

piatkus

PIATKUS

First published in the US in 2015
First published in Great Britain in 2015 by Piatkus

1 3 5 7 9 10 8 6 4 2

A CIP catalogue record for this book
is available from the British Library.

ISBN 978-0-349-40718-0

Typeset in Adobe Garamond by M Rules
Printed and bound in Great Britain by
Clays Ltd, St Ives plc.

Papers used by Piatkus are from well-managed forests
and other responsible sources.

To The Cupertino A Team

Harry, Mark, Dave, Rog, Xabi, and Art

Thank you for your unmatched wisdom and awesomeness. This book wouldn't have been the same without you! By the way, remember that one time *I* saved *you* from a fire?

Just sayin' . . .

Chapter 1

I took a deep breath and sipped my soda. It was in a red plastic cup, so the party patrol, aka my best friend Harper, wouldn't know that I, once again, wasn't partaking in the festivities. This was the third social gathering she'd dragged me to in two weeks, and though I appreciated her help of 'trying to get my ass in gear and out of this depression,' I still wasn't happy.

Jack had left a month ago. Actually, it was four weeks and three endless days ago, and no matter how many times I was told it would get easier, it still hurt to breathe past the pain. Sometimes I held my breath as long as I could, just to escape the jagged edges of my heart tearing through my chest. But tonight was supposed to be different, a distraction, Harper had promised. It was Halloween, the one time of year people get to make believe they're someone else. Someone stronger or faster or sexier or smarter – or braver. Someone whole. Despite the red cape and title of Riding Hood, I couldn't escape the devastating fact that I was still me . . . And all the baggage that came with.

'Lana!' Harper shouted, shimmying toward me through the massive amount of people. I could hear her sexy police officer costume squeaking and squishing as she approached. 'Isn't this place great?' she said, standing by me and adjusting the cuffs at her hip. She took a drink from her own cup. Judging by the smell, it was only partially soda – the more dominant part was tequila.

'Yeah, it's a really nice house.'

Rhett Simpson was one of the firefighters who worked at the station across the street from our house. He'd had his eye on Harper for a while. Though she was relatively secretive when it came to her dating life, I'd managed to figure out that Harper had a couple firemen on her hook, but I had no idea if she was actually into any of them. She was the queen of casual and always had a backup guy, a safety line to keep her from ever getting close enough for a real relationship. Advice she'd once given me and I should have taken. Maybe then I wouldn't be standing here, surrounded by people, feeling completely alone. Out of place.

The house was packed with people in costume, most of whom either worked for or frequented the firehouse, and Harper was getting a lot of looks.

'Did you come as a police officer just to piss off the gaggle of firemen you know?' I asked.

She flicked an invisible hair from her costume and shrugged. 'Might have.'

Police officers and firemen apparently had their own ideas about which branch was better. And Harper was great at playing the devil's advocate. She was the kind of woman a man had to work to get. I loved her. I wished I had whatever gene she carried that was encoded with charisma.

I took another drink of my soda, wishing there was something stronger in it.

'So . . . ' she smiled and danced a little. The tequila was obviously working well for her. 'Are you having fun?'

'Mmm hmmm,' I said with a forced smiled. 'I don't think I'm going to stay too late, though. I have a meeting with my thesis advisor on Monday, and—'

'And it's Saturday night.'

'I just want to go over a few more things on my proposal.' I was presenting the rough draft for my project the day after tomorrow, and school was the one thing going well in my life. Sure, I had to maintain a high GPA to keep my scholarship, but it was more than that. Throwing myself into this project kept my mind busy and my goals in sight.

Harper sighed, put her drink down on the nearby table, and cupped my shoulder.

'I love you, damn it,' she said.

I blinked twice. 'I know. I love you too.'

'Then tell me what it's going to take to snap you out of this. Jack is gone. He left. You haven't heard from him in a month, and even though it's your favorite holiday and you look amazing, you're walking around like a zombie. Which I would have happily done your make up for. Red Riding Hood zombie sounds kind of awesome, now that I think about it.' She smiled and rubbed my arms. 'But I hate seeing you like this.'

'This coming from the person who doesn't tell me anything about what's going on in her love life?' I asked.

She glanced down, and I felt instantly horrible.

'I'm sorry, Harp. I just ... I feel like everyone else has secrets. Gets to hide what they want to hide, feel how they want to feel, and maybe I just want that too?'

She frowned. 'Wallowing is different than feeling. And I'm not trying to hide things from you. My relationship status is tricky, and when I figure it out, I'll talk to you about it.'

'Fine.'

Harper had always been this way. She had to figure things out first. She had to be in control. Funny how I seemed to gravitate toward that type of person in my life. Yes, I knew she cared about me, I just hated that sometimes I was the one who seemed to always need advice. That was, until Jack. I had a better idea now of what to expect from men.

3

And that was nothing.

Harper had been right. Giving away your heart and trust was dangerous, and I learned the hard way.

'Why don't you have a drink and—'

'No,' I said quickly. Because it hit me then what kind of person I was. And what kind of people were drawn to me. 'I get it,' I said to Harper. 'I know you like things your way, on your terms. I know you need control, but I'm not the pawn.'

Her eyes went wide. 'Lana, I've never thought of you that way. I just want to help.'

I closed my eyes for a moment. 'I know. But . . .' I had a hard time with people 'wanting to help.' Maybe I was being harsh on Harper. The truth was blaring in my face, and I couldn't ignore it anymore. 'I just need to be in control of my life. On my own. Does that make sense?'

She nodded. 'Yes. I'm sorry. I know I can be quick to tell you what your problem is.'

I smiled. 'And sometimes I need to hear it. But now that this whole mess with Jack and my dad and Brock is done, I'm taking control back. Not giving it up.'

She nodded. 'That's good.'

'And I know Jack's not coming back. I've made peace with that.' Which was the truth. I was focused on grad school, at least trying to focus. Sure, I was a having an issue with insomnia lately, and the lack of sleep wasn't helping my brain. There was also this gaping hole in my chest that wouldn't go away . . .

Maybe Harper was right. Maybe I was a zombie.

'Have you really made peace with that?' she asked softly.

'I'm trying,' I said. 'I've spent the last month trying.' Trying not to think of Jack. Trying to not recall how he shattered me in every way possible. Trying not to remember how his back looked when he turned it on me and walked away.

4

He'd helped me find strength. Even though Brock was still in Denver, living with my dad and Anita, I hadn't heard from them. I'd caught wind that my father was traveling to the New York branch of his firm on a regular basis. But, when and for how long, I didn't know.

Realizing where my father's loyalty lay, and that it wasn't with me, had stung, but deep inside, I'd already known. Had known for a while. The incident with Jack just helped me realize it and let go of a silly dream that would never come true. My father would never pick me over my step-brother, and he'd never believe me. Even worse, he'd never believe in me. For now, Brock was twenty miles away and in a city I didn't go to, now that school was in session. I was off their radar, and I could be left alone.

Jack had helped me do that. Helped me deal with issues from my past and move on. He'd taken control when I needed it, only to leave me to figure out who I was without him, or his tight rein. Hilarious thing was, I may have dealt with the past, but I had new baggage to carry.

And his name was Jack Powell.

Instead of healing, I simply traded in one issue for a new model. I was alone. He was gone.

Gone, gone, gone.

The pain had subsided some, but the emptiness was still very present. A new emotion was taking over. Anger. I was past sad. Past wrecked. Past trying to understand or figure out where or how or why. I was just angry.

And hollow.

Gotta love the stages of grief.

'Well, I'm glad you're trying, and I will also try to not be so . . . bitchy.' She winked. 'Or controlling. But you do know I just want to help, right?'

I nodded. 'I do know that.'

5

'Great!' she said. 'Then let's continue trying, because I miss your smile,' Harper brushed the cape of my costume off my shoulders, revealing my peasant shirt and cincher. 'The girls look great tonight!' she said, glancing at my chest, then spinning toward the mass of people mingling in the large entertainment room. It was never my goal to go as 'sexy red riding hood,' which was why I made my own costume. Hence the long red skirt. But, yeah, my boobs were a bit on display, which wasn't my intention. Not much I could do with a D cup, though, which was the reason I was hiding behind the cape.

'What exactly are we trying for?' a husky voice came from behind me. I knew that voice. The damn thing gave me shivers since the moment I'd first heard it, and every time after.

I turned to find Callum Malone in all his costume glory of . . .

'You're dressed as a fire fighter,' I said. Not that I was complaining. The man was tall, all muscle, and filled out his fire gear like no one's business. His blues eyes burned bright as he looked me over, effectively leaving hot chills. Yep, the administering of hot chills must be something he learned in fire school. Which was one of the reasons I'd avoided him this past month.

He glanced down the front of him. 'You don't like my costume, Kitten?'

'It's your profession, so it doesn't count as a costume.'

'Halloween is the one time you get to be someone else,' Harper said with a smile, tossing a hand on her hip, showcasing her police getup.

Cal looked at her. 'And I see you chose to dress as a pain in the ass.'

'Funny,' she said, adjusting her badge.

He took a step closer, the smell of spice and man and heavy material that had been in smoke and fire notched my internal temperature up several degrees.

6

'Why dress up like someone else?' he responded to Harper, but looked at me. 'When the night is done, I'm still me, and that's something everyone deals with. May as well embrace it from the beginning.'

I swallowed hard. There was more to that statement than the surface words he'd used. Cal was Jack's best friend and knew what I'd gone through with Jack. The basic details at least. I'm sure he was also aware that I was hiding from him because he made me ...

Well, he made me feel things.

Things like hope. Maybe even hope for something better than the dull ache and fury that had recently taken me over. Which was stupid. Going down any kind of path, with any kind of man, with any kind of hope, was just flat stupid.

I had made my decision. I was seeking my own control. Not another person.

Cal's eyes paused on my chest, then he smiled and met my face. 'While embodying a different persona is not my gig, I'm changing my stance on dressing up. You should wear that corset whenever you want.'

Harper rolled her eyes, and I put the cape back over my shoulders. Not because I minded him glancing at me, but because I didn't want him to see those shivers he made me feel break over my skin. Cal was the only man who'd had that effect on me since Jack, which was annoying, since he and Jack were as close as brothers.

Harper looked at the crowd and someone caught her eye. 'Well, you two chat, I'll just be over there,' she said, and patted my shoulder. 'Have fun.'

Fun? Cal was the epitome of fun, but he was also hard to be around. Because every time I looked at him, my mind wondered about things it shouldn't. Things like timing. Like 'what ifs' that ranged from 'what if I'd met him before Jack,' or 'what if his muscles were as hard as they looked' and 'what if I bit his bicep—'

I had to stop that line of thinking.

Cal was Jack's best friend, and Jack was my ex. A hard term I was still learning to say. By a freak chance of fate, I had kissed both of them in the same week. But that was months ago. Since then, I'd found out that Cal was at the bar the night I met Jack. And it was that night I kept rethinking – reliving. Because, while I hadn't known the two men knew each other, they both had been at the same place, the same time I was. And that night could have gone one of a million directions.

But it hadn't.

I had laid eyes on Jack first.

However, it was more recently that I'd discovered the reason I didn't see Cal was because he'd stopped the man who almost knocked my table over.

That's when Jack had come to the rescue . . .

Nope. I had to remind myself once again I was not going there. Trying to figure out all the missed opportunities, the moments and experiences and instances that could have gone differently only left me feeling more hollow and angry. I didn't need more crap to deal with, since one specific emotion was driving me crazy.

Lust.

I'd gotten a taste of candy, and now couldn't get the sugar off my tongue.

My body was recently awakened to sex, so now I knew what I was missing. Knew what it meant to feel good. Actually, it had been better than good. I'd felt alive and wanted. Yes, Jack had been the main source of my needs – and fulfilling them – but there was one moment, one kiss with Cal that still lingered. That hot memory of his mouth, his warmth and strength as he surrounded me.

Another thought I should extinguish, but couldn't bring myself to do it.

I was looking for a way to vent my rage, while running as fast as I could in the other direction. I didn't want to be around people, not because my anxiety was bad, but because I didn't give a shit. Funny how destroying someone's trust and faith in love could do that. My body, however, was going through some kind of touch withdrawal. The whole situation made for a perfect storm of crankiness.

But Cal? Despite knowing better, he was the only man who made me wonder . . . what if?

'You're looking at me like I just kicked your dog,' he said.

I glanced down, my face relaxing. I must have been scowling hard. 'Sorry, just thoughts.'

'Care to share them?'

No, not really. But in the spirit of anger and emptiness, I was considering it. Because not much rattled me lately. I had school that I cared about. And Harper. But no more family, no more budding career, no more Jack.

'I'm just not in the mood.'

He lifted a brow. 'That's pretty vague.'

My eyes snapped to his with heated anger. Jack's words drifted through my memory:

You know I hate vagueness . . .

'Fine, you want something direct?' I asked sharply.

'Yes, please.'

'I hate this.' There, that was direct. 'When I say I'm not in the mood, what I mean is I don't want to be here. I don't want to try to have fun. I don't even want to be me, something the costume was supposed to help with, and it's not.' Realization made me choke on the last word. Because he stared at me with hard determination and a soft understanding all at the same time.

'I don't want to think about things. I don't want you to think about things, and I don't even want you standing there,' I waved my hand over his general direction, 'Looking like that.'

His perfect mouth pursed, and he nodded like I had a point. Which I didn't. I was just pissed and rambling. Hating the fact that one phrase he spoke reminded me of Jack. Reminded me they were friends. Reminded me of all the ways I'd come up lacking, and all the reasons he could have stayed, but chose to leave.

Never again.

I couldn't be that weak again. I was certain my body couldn't physically take it. Jack had wanted control, and I'd given it. It was my turn to control my world now. I just wasn't sure how to do that, outside of giving into the burning feeling and popping off at the mouth.

'Fair enough,' he said, humoring me and taking off his helmet. 'Before I start stripping, though, you could clarify what it is you want me to look like, if not this?'

'I don't want you to strip,' I said. Which was half a lie. Okay, it was more than half, because the man was sexy as sin, and the idea of him taking his clothes off made my entire core throb and anticipation race through my system so hard my veins were vibrating.

'You said you didn't want me looking like this?'

'That's not what I meant.' And he knew it. But he was so good at making things casual and easy.

'Ouch, Kitten. You know, I've got the outfit ...' He set his helmet down and started to take off the jacket exaggeratedly slowly.

'Yeow! Malone is putting on a show!' a fellow firefighter dressed as James Bond shouted and turned up the music.

'Hey, this is a private party over here,' he said over his shoulder, then faced me again to wink.

I shielded my face and shook my head.

'Hey, you said—'

'I know what I said,' I groaned. Leave it to Cal to try to take my mind off things. Same as he'd been trying to do since Jack left. Except for the fact that I'd been avoiding him.

He put his jacket next to his helmet on the table, leaving him in his pants with the red suspenders hanging down and a tight white T-shirt. Every muscle and ridge was defined, and those poor cotton sleeves could barely contain his biceps.

He ushered me to the nearest corner for some kind of privacy. At least I didn't have to see anyone over his towering build and massive shoulders. He was like a—

My throat closed again.

Wall.

He was like a wall.

Just like Jack had been the first night I met him.

But Cal wasn't Jack. I didn't want him to be. Because, wall or not, and similarities aside, there were still large differences. It pinged my chest every time a twist of something familiar came out from Cal. And he had no idea. He couldn't know what my mind was doing to me, but he let me babble and be pissy with him anyway.

'Can you at least tell me what things you don't want me to think about?' he asked, referring to my earlier statement.

His blue eyes were like an ocean at dawn, and I wanted to tell him exactly what I was thinking. That I hated how I felt inside. Hated that this hollowness followed me everywhere, and I couldn't beat it. Hated that every time I looked at Cal or was in his presence, were the only times I felt remotely warm.

I didn't want to think about any of it.

But him? 'Mostly, I just don't want you thinking I'm broken.'

His expression turned serious. 'Kitten, you're far from broken.'

His words rolled off his tongue so genuinely, it actually made me believe him. 'But, since I'm not allowed to think in your presence, I won't tell you that while I generally disagree with your pal Harper, she's on to something in trying to get you to move.'

'I've moved on,' I defended quickly.

'I didn't say move *on*. That may never happen.'

His honesty hit like a slap in the face. He'd called out my lie, because no, I hadn't totally moved on from Jack. And, truthfully, he'd just confirmed my greatest fear that I may never.

'Consider just moving in a different direction.' His voice was raspy, and I realized it was because, at some point, he'd gotten closer. My nose almost brushed his chest as I looked up into his eyes.

'And what direction might that be?' I asked, my own voice a little thick.

The sexiest grin a man could ever be blessed with split his face.

'One far away from here.'

I tried to breathe, but instead, his scent engulfed me and made my senses go haywire. That lust I'd been fighting? It was not playing nice right now. It wasn't about just having sex, it was about connection. I missed being touched. Missed feeling skin against mine. Sex used to be an ugly, terrifying notion to me. But it had been repackaged as beautiful and intimate – and damn it, I missed it.

Minus the intimacy.

I didn't want to get caught up in feelings again, because it hurt way too much when the curtain fell, the bliss was over, and all that was left was a soul-deep kind of freeze that cracked my bones.

No . . . no intimacy.

But touch?

My hands itched to do just that.

'You said you didn't want to be here,' Cal rasped. 'I can take you away. Say yes and I'll do that.'

I swallowed hard. Did I want Cal to take me away? *Yes.* But saying it out loud made it more concrete, gave the feelings I'd chosen to ignore power. 'I have to tell Harper I'm leaving first.'

'Okay,' he said and moved aside. I glanced around the house of people and couldn't find her.

'Let me look for her, I'll meet you by the front door. Wait for me there.'

'Yes ma'am,' Cal said with a smile. When he said it like that, I realized that I'd just given an order. Huh. Interesting. And not an entirely bad feeling. In fact, it was kind of surprising how much I liked the authoritative tone in my voice.

I wove through a bunch of people, looking for Harper. I peeked out the window – no one on the back porch either. I went upstairs, then turned down the hall and called out her name.

Nothing.

A low muffled sound was coming from one of the rooms. The door was slightly open, so I tapped lightly.

'Harper?' I asked and looked in. She was bent over the bed while someone in a Viking costume fucked her from behind. I gasped and shut the door.

There was a string of quiet curses, followed by Harper adjusting her costume as she came out and glared at me.

'Sorry,' I said. 'I didn't mean to barge in, I just wanted you to know I was thinking of leaving.'

'Oh,' she said, breathing heavily. 'With who?'

'Cal is going to give me a ride home.'

She nodded. Now wasn't the time to ask what was going on or who she was with. I hadn't been able to see his face, and couldn't recall who came in a Viking costume. It technically wasn't my business anyway. But I still cared about Harper. She was my best friend, and we had come here together.

'Are you going to be okay getting home?'

She smiled and glanced over her shoulder. 'Yeah, I'm all good.'

I nodded and hustled away. Yep, not the time or the place. She was doing her thing and, apparently, that thing was a Viking, so . . . if that wasn't my cue to exit, nothing was.

As I walked downstairs, I saw Cal standing by the door, just like I'd asked, rather told. A small flare of warmth lit me up. I was in control. At least attempting to be.

Chapter 2

Cal put his truck in park and killed the engine. Coming around the front, he opened my door and helped me out, then grabbed the six pack of beer he'd 'borrowed' from his friend's party and walked toward the tailgate.

'God, it's beautiful out here,' I said, taking a deep breath of fresh air. It was chilly, but clear and bright. Cal had taken a back road that led to a small pond with a great view of the Colorado wilderness as a backdrop.

'Yeah, whenever I'm *not in the mood*, I usually come out here,' he winked.

Though he was using my words from earlier, I was still curious to ask, 'Why?'

'Perspective. See over there where the woods are?'

I looked in the direction he pointed and frowned. 'You mean those few sticks that look like they once were trees?'

'Yep, those. There was a forest fire several years back. It was the first call I went on.' He popped a beer open, took one quick drink, then handed it to me.

'That must have been intense,' I said, squinting to see more of what was left of the forest. While the grand scene was something that could be plastered on the cover of National Geographic, there was this one blemish of what once was. A forest that once thrived was off in the distance. It was hard to see, especially in the dark, but it was there.

'It was.' Moonlight reflected off the pond and lit his face so well that I could see every small expression and angle of his lips as he spoke. 'I was scared as hell and so fucking excited at the same time.'

I took a sip of beer. The cold glass bottle chilled my upper lip as I drank a long swallow down.

'Well, you were running into something you knew would burn you. That would be scary.'

'And exciting,' he repeated that last word. 'It was also sad seeing all the devastation it left behind.' His shoulder brushed mine as he reached out, gently took the beer, and took another drink before handing it back. 'Could have been a lot worse, though. It was the only time I thought I wasn't going to make it out.'

'What?' I said in shock.

He just chuckled. Chuckled! Like him almost dying in a fire was 'just another day.'

'I was younger, trained, but still a rookie. A tree fell and the fire spread really fast and surrounded me.'

'So, you just come out here, look at this place, and remember?'

'Yeah, because I have to.'

'No, you don't,' I said softly. Remembering the bad stuff sounded like a terrible idea to me, yet Cal had a different opinion when it came to this.

'People run into things they know will burn them all the time,' he said. His words hit me hard and the pain in my chest redoubled, thinking of Jack. I'd ran fast and blind into him, and knew the whole time he was an inferno I couldn't control.

'I learned a lot,' Cal continued. 'Like how to handle myself better for next time. That's why I come out here. To remember the pain, the adrenaline, and the fear. All of it gave me tools to be better.'

I bit the inside of my cheek and fidgeted with the beer in my hand. 'That's a good lesson,' I admitted. 'And I'm glad you brought me here. I'm glad you're okay.'

I handed him the bottle once more, my hand was now freezing, having clasped the bottle for so long, and I rubbed them together quickly.

'You warm enough?' he asked, opening the tailgate.

'I'm alright, the cape is pretty heavy.'

Cal, however, was wearing only a T-shirt and fireman's pants. While it was a great look for him, he couldn't be that warm.

'What about you?' I asked.

'Yeah, I'm good. I tend to run hot.'

I nodded, having no doubt about that. Without warning, he grabbed my waist, his big hands sliding around my hips as he lifted me up to sit on the tailgate. I gasped a little at the surprise of his touch. No matter how brief it was. He sat me down, then stood in front of me. I shivered a little because, even in the dark, with the glow of the taillights illuminating the night, I could see his blue eyes roam across my body like he was searching for something.

He'd looked at me the same way the night I'd met him. He had a way of effortlessly making me feel seen, inspiring a soul-deep heat that caused my mind to crank out the memory of his lips, and how amazing they felt against mine.

'I'm not buying it, Kitten,' he finally said. Before I could ask more, he left me sitting there, grabbed something from the cab of the truck, then came back. 'Here.' He wrapped his fire jacket over my shoulders. The smell of spice and the feel of the rough material instantly engulfed me, and I took another deep breath.

Wide open space, stars, and wrapped in Cal's jacket made me feel déjà vu. I remembered the time Jack had wrapped me in his coat when I'd first met him.

I closed my eyes and hung my head. It was like Cal and Jack were connected on some cosmic level.

'What's wrong?' he asked, putting his hands on either side of my hips, grabbing the edge of the tailgate.

I shook my head. 'I feel like this is some cruel game.'

'What do you mean?'

I laughed, but there was nothing funny about this situation. 'I don't know what I mean. It sounds crazy.'

'I can deal with crazy.' He stepped a little closer until my dangling shins met his thighs. 'Tell me.' The deep rough sound of his voice was something I'd never heard before. It was a command. Casual, easygoing Cal was obviously alpha, but this was the first time I'd ever heard the dominance come out. I tried hard not to respond, but my entire body wouldn't listen.

'Everything feels like a repeat,' I said, and glanced at his face. 'Jack left, and it hurts. Still hurts. But you are his friend and there are similarities.'

He frowned, but took another small step closer, shifting his hips, and silently urging me to continue. So I did. No reason not to be honest.

'There are certain things you say, how you move ... even giving me your jacket. Those moments just remind me of him. How we met. Words he said to me once.'

Cal took a rough breath that seemed to be lined with less than thrilled intent.

'It's never fun being compared to another man,' he said.

I hung my head, but he cupped my neck and made me face him. His touch was warm, and felt so good against my skin. Once upon a time, I'd associated it with a dirty thing, but now I craved it. Missed it. Longed for the skin to skin connection. It was like a drug.

'I want you to really hear what I'm saying, Lana,' Cal started. His eyes bored into mine. 'I'm not Jack.'

'I know,' I said quickly, and dismissed it because yeah, that was obvious.

'No.' He held firm. 'I'm. Not. Jack.'

I studied him for a long time. Anger and angst rolled off of him. But there was understanding too. Some kind of patience I couldn't quite put my finger on, but I felt it in how he touched me.

'I'm not Jack,' he said once more, 'And I'm not going to be your dark corner either.'

I frowned. But he went on.

'I know Jack hurt you, and yes, he's my best friend. I know what's ahead of me when it comes to you, and it's not going to be easy. We may have some common ground, but we're different people. If you want to hide, I can't help with that or allow it.' His thumb traced my cheekbone. 'But if you want to run? Fight? Feel something?' One more step and my legs had to spread slightly to welcome him into my space. 'That's my department all day long.'

His sly grin was sexy but serious, and made me want to do all those things at the same time. Run away, fight with him, feel something. Because there was an anger deep in me too. And I wanted to unleash it.

He was right, though. The shadow that had served as my protection, my hideout, had been Jack. The corner of my world that he had sheltered and controlled. That carried heat and a safe place that pushed my limits to accept my strength.

But that wasn't Cal.

'It's up to you, Lana. But understand that whatever is going on, whatever shit you need to work out regarding Jack, I'm here. I want to hear about it.'

'I'm mad,' I whispered. 'I feel like I'm not the same person I was.'

'Because you're not. But that doesn't have to be a bad thing.'

19

I shook my head. This whole moment was ridiculous. Thinking of Jack, talking about it, was something I avoided. Because his memory did what it always did.

It upset me and made me realize for the millionth time that my strength had come with a price. I've given away part of myself. Trusted him. Loved him. And he healed a piece of my heart. He also took that part with him when he left.

I may be less than I was, but I was stronger. And I was not interested in letting someone else exercise their needs over me. Once upon a time, I'd liked it. Liked how I was taken over. Craved it even.

Not anymore. It was my time to exercise my needs. And I *needed* to stop feeling. Stop the hollow pain that was taking over.

'It is up to me,' I said in a low tone I didn't recognize. 'And I don't want to feel any of this.'

If I was going to feel something, damn it, it would be something good. And it wouldn't have anything to do with Jack or his memory. It would be mine. My actions. My emotions. My control.

Cal stared at me hard. 'What do you see when you look at me?'

The question was so blunt, so honest, I couldn't escape it. I gazed into his blue eyes and wondered for the thousandth time what my life would have been like if I'd met Cal first. So many doubts and unknowns. But in that moment, the answer to his question was suddenly clear.

'I see my next mistake.'

Without thinking, I grabbed his shirt in my fist, and kissed him hard.

His hand slipped to my nape and he pulled me into him until my lips mashed further against his. I moaned, instantly recognizing him from all those months ago. But this time it wasn't soft, it was heavy and intoxicating. His free arm wrapped around my waist and pulled me into him, my legs spreading wide until my skirt bunched enough to give room for him to be flush against me.

Every part of him was hard, strong, and surrounded me. I didn't reach out, didn't cling to him the way I wanted, because that would be too much. I wouldn't reach out for anyone again. It wasn't a smart action, and I'd learned that reaching only gave room for them to pull away.

So, I kissed him, keeping my hand locked on the center of his chest, grabbing only the soft cotton there. I leaned in as he worked his mouth over mine, his tongue seeking and dueling. He pulled me even closer. The thick material of his fire pants scratched the insides of my thighs, and God damn, it felt good. Even better was his hardening cock that hit just the right spot and had me seeing stars behind my closed eyes.

I bit his lip and thrust my tongue hard. Deeper. The wantonness that lay dormant in me was rousing. With every touch, every taste, I awakened a little more. Wanted more. Wanted *him*.

His stubble rubbed against my chin, delivering a delicious sting as he dove his tongue in deep, tasting everything I was. I itched to wrap my arms around him and pull him closer.

But I stayed strong. Kept my distance.

He plunged again, and it felt like his mouth was showing exactly what his body could do to mine. He retreated to bite my bottom lip, then thrust deep once more. The burn of his skin against mine and the consuming way he kissed me was dizzying.

I pulled back, and on a heavy breath asked, 'Do you ever wonder what would have happened if you hadn't gotten called to a fire the night we met?'

'Every damn day.'

My scalp prickled and my throat closed up. He thought about it. Just as much, maybe more than I did. But where did that leave us?

The past carried so much weight, I didn't know what to do with it. Because it didn't matter. Our paths had been set. Played out how they were supposed to. And now I sat with Jack's memory and Cal's body both equally invading my space, and I couldn't, wouldn't, reach out for either.

If there was one thing I'd learned, it was that I had some kind of control, and I refused to be weak. Refused to hope, or feel, for something deeper than surface, because when it was gone, it hurt. It hurt so bad that I could still feel a ripped piece of flesh from bones, leaving me half a person.

Cal may not think I was broken, but I was suffering from a direct hit and damage that may never fully heal.

'I should get home,' I whispered, feeling as though I was on the brink of messing with fate once again.

Chapter 3

'I think this is a great start,' Erica Keys said, looking at my thesis proposal. She was in her mid-to-late thirties and a wonderful thesis advisor. She was also a wonderful human being. I respected her because she'd fought hard to get into the position she was in. Earning a full professorship at her age was no small feat. She also seemed to genuinely care about her students and their success.

Our meetings were later in the evening, and after a full day of classes, I'd walked into her office and she insisted we go to the campus coffee shop.

'Thank you again for inviting me out,' I said. Though the café was only on the other side of the parking lot from the college, it was a nice change in scenery.

'You looked like you could use some caffeine,' she said.

That was the truth. Between this newest bout of insomnia and school, I felt permanently exhausted.

'One hazelnut latte?' the waiter said with a steaming cup of heavenly smelling java.

'That's me,' I answered, and he put the large cup in front of me, the foam gently swaying side to side, making the heart-shaped design dance.

'And a chai tea,' he put that in front of Erica before walking off.

'He's cute,' she said, wiggling her eyebrows at me.

'I um ... what?'

She hid her grin by taking a quick drink of her tea. 'The waiter is cute, and he was looking at you. Are you single? If so, you should go for him.'

A flare of awkwardness skated up my back. Not because of Erica. Though she was my thesis advisor, she was young and treated me like an equal and a friend. Which I really liked. It was the 'are you single?' question that tied up my tongue. Mostly because my tongue had been tied a couple days ago with a firefighter's.

'I'm not really in the market to date,' I answered. Though, technically, I was single. 'Are you in cahoots with Harper?' I asked jokingly.

'Who's Harper?'

'She's my friend. She's been saying similar things. Trying to get me out, to date, things like that.'

'Well, you should listen to her,' Erica said, and tilted her head toward the counter. 'Because waiter boy is still staring at you.'

I glanced over and, oh boy, he smiled and gave one of those chin lift things. My cheeks heated instantly.

Erica was obviously loving this.

'Not my type,' I said quickly, and cupped my mug in both palms.

'Well, you should still find something to do besides school. Go out and have fun once in a while.'

'I do.'

Erica gave me a disbelieving look. 'Lana, I'm your advisor, I've seen your class schedule. Are you trying to take every class Golden has to offer in one term, or is taking forty-thousand credits and working on your thesis fun for you?'

'Hey now,' I defended. 'It's only thirty thousand credits and yes, it's quite fun.'

'Uh-huh, well it's healthy to have a social life. You know that thing that takes place outside of school.'

'Oh, I see now, this coffee date was all a set up.'

'Yep,' Erica said with no shame. 'I have officially gotten you to be social with at least me for a short time. Your psyche can thank me later.'

I laughed and took a drink of hazelnut yumminess. In all honesty, this was nice. Getting out of school and chatting. The smell of roasted coffee beans combined with the soft glow of the shop made my shoulders relax. It was far from the florescent lights of my last lecture hall and maybe Erica was right, maybe getting out of the college from time to time was a good thing.

'Well, I suppose we should get a little accomplished,' she said, pulling her trendy glasses from her head to her face, her attention going back to my proposal in front of her. She took one sip and went back to reading through the draft spread out on the table. Her sensible heels clicked under the table in a slow, tap, tap, tap, as she flipped another page, then another.

I started sweating a little.

'I'm still working through some ideas . . .' I started, then trailed off. I needed to let her read it before I started freaking out. Which was difficult, because sitting across from someone while they silently looked over your work was agony.

'Working ideas or not, this is the most thorough rough draft I've ever seen.' She smiled at me. 'It's clear you worked hard on this, and it's going to be great.'

Tucking a lock of short brown hair behind her ear, she swung her glasses back to the top of her head and intertwined her fingers before resting them on my paper. She was simple and lovely and didn't have to try.

'What do you think about going a step further? I know statistics is your area of focus, but you're interested in finance, right?'

'Yes. I eventually want to be a financial analyst.'

'Okay, so you want to work with businesses and advise them

25

on how to invest their money and how to keep their business strong, right?'

'Yes.'

'Then I think bringing in a real world experience would be great. We need to present a really strong case to the thesis board, and I think perhaps some insight into an actual business would be beneficial.'

I tossed her words around in my mind for a moment. It was Erica's job to help me make the strongest project possible, and she would then stamp her approval on it and take it to the thesis board. Her support was basically gold.

'What do you mean take it a step further?' I asked.

She glanced at my paper. 'Since you haven't had experience in an actual financial firm, I think the board would love to see how you could apply the methods you've outlined to an actual business.'

I folded my lips because, while I had left out the part about my father owning a financial firm, I also didn't mention that I had worked there for a heartbeat this past summer. That was, until I started doing payroll for Jack's resort. Yeah, all that I left out. Because I wanted this to be my thing. Start to finish, my project, with no mention or even hint of anyone else. Problem was, the only two people I knew who owned businesses were Jack and my father. Both of whom I couldn't go to, even if I wanted to. Which I didn't.

'I think getting an inside look at how a company is run will help flesh out your thesis. This is a great start,' she tapped my paper, 'But if you could shadow a business owner, see how they keep themselves in the black, it would benefit you and your project greatly.'

Shadowing the owner of a company. Trying to get an interview was one thing, but shadowing? If I Googled 'business owner in

Denver,' how long it would take to find a corporation, get an appointment with the head of it, much less an interview, then get to Denver, since there were no real 'big business execs' in Golden.

'With the holidays coming up, it may be hard to shadow a big business owner anytime soon,' I admitted.

'Oh, it doesn't have to be a big business,' she said. 'Just someone who owns their own and has some success. I'm sure there are a bunch here in Golden. You don't have to think skyscraper VP's.'

Funny how my mind had gone there on its own. But it was a relief to not need that kind of company. Also a relief I didn't have to go into Denver. Erica did have a good idea, though. Only problem was – who was I supposed to shadow? Instead of worrying too much about that now, I smiled and nodded. 'I can do that.'

Erica smiled back and handed me my paper. 'Great!'

She took another pull of her tea and motioned toward the counter again. 'Now, let's get back to this other business at hand. You going to leave your number for the cute waiter?'

I tried not to choke on the last long gulp of my latte. 'I don't think so.'

Erica shrugged. 'Well, maybe next time. I know of a lot of coffee shops in the area.'

'Can't wait,' I said, and thanked her for her advice. Getting up, I put on my coat and turned to walk out.

'Your work ethic is impressive, and I'm anxious to see what you bring me next,' she said with so much support in her voice it made my shoulders feel a little lighter.

'Thank you. I'll see you next week.'

I headed across the street toward the side parking lot by my lecture building. It was already dark, since the class was in the early evening and the winter months were right around the corner. There were only a few scattered lamps and my car sitting alone in the far corner of the lot.

I took a deep breath of chilly air and smiled. That had gone perfectly, better than perfect, and it was all me. School was the one thing that was solely mine. And I had just nailed it. My success wasn't reliant on my family name or Jack's controlling reach . . .

I tried not to think of Jack.

Or Cal.

Or kissing Cal the other night.

Everything outside my little academia bubble was chaotic. Feelings, expectations, a shattered soul . . . it was all tough to deal with, so I tried not to. Tried not to replay how Cal's lips felt against mine. Or how he stated plainly what he was and, more importantly, what he wasn't.

And he wasn't Jack. But I also wasn't the same Lana that Cal had met a few months ago. The 'what ifs' and 'timing' didn't matter because life moved how it did.

Wondering how different my life may be if he'd gotten to me before Jack didn't help anything.

'Gotten to me?' I scoffed at my own word choice as I continued the long walk to my car. Then again, I guess that's what it felt like. Jack had swooped me up before I knew what was happening. But I'd liked it, and I fell hard.

And Cal? He'd been there. From the beginning. And I wanted to know so much what the alternative may have been. What it felt like to be wrapped in Cal's arms . . .

A shadow moved by my car, snagging my attention and stopping me in my tracks. Someone was standing next to it.

The figure was too small to be Cal. Not that I expected him to show up.

But it was definitely a man. Bigger than me, and in a dark trench coat. The shadows hid his face. He took a step in my direction. Fear enveloped me, but I beat it back. When the man

28

stepped into the light, I swallowed down the familiar taste of horror I'd grown accustomed to.

Brock. The step-brother from hell who hurt me when I was young and, to this day, took enjoyment from my fear.

'Is there a reason you're lurking around my car?' I asked.

He stepped toward me. I was determined not to be afraid. He still creeped me out, but the more I let him have that power over me, the more he won. And the more he'd continue to impact my life. I was done letting him have *any* impact on me whatsoever. I'd found some strength over the past few months. I could control my world to a point. And I wouldn't let Brock chase me from anything.

'I thought this was yours. Just thought I'd stop by and say hi.'

'All the way from Denver, huh?'

He lifted a shoulder. 'I have reasons for being in Golden.'

I shook my head. 'I'm done playing this game with you. You don't scare me.'

He laughed. 'Aw, sis, what makes you think I want to scare you?'

Because you're a sociopath who takes joy in my fear and have since day one.

'Just stay away from me,' I said with all the confidence I felt, and pushed past him to unlock my car.

He had hurt me once, I wouldn't let him hurt me again. Showing up here to spook me may have worked in the past, but not now. I wouldn't be the mouse he toyed with anymore. I may not be able to prove it, and some people might not believe me, but I knew the truth, and that was enough. It had to be.

I got in my car, shut the door, immediately locked it, and then started the engine.

'You drive safe now,' he said loudly, so I could hear through the rolled up windows. With a sinister smile, he watched as I pulled away. My only wish was that I could have run over his foot in the process, because he looked like he'd already won some victory over me.

I sat in my car, angry that my hands were still shaking. I was home, safe, but I wasn't ready to go in. I wasn't ready to tell Harper about my day. I needed to get it together first and smother this sick feeling rising in my stomach.

I hit my palms against the steering wheel.

They still didn't stop shaking, so I tried again. And again.

Go away! My mind yelled. Screaming for peace.

Go away!

All of it. The pain of Jack leaving. The knowledge that Brock may never leave me alone. The shred of fear, unease, that still lingered in my veins. I just wanted all of it to go away.

I hit my hands against the steering wheel one more time, my breath coming fast, and I screamed, 'Go. Away!'

A light tap came on my window, and I jumped.

'Whoa, Kitten, take it easy on the Honda,' Cal said. 'I can go away, but your poor car looks like it's being attacked.'

A humorous scoff escaped. I rolled down my window. 'And you couldn't possibly walk away knowing an innocent Honda was being attacked?'

Placing a hand on the top of my car, he leaned down, his Golden Fire Department issued blue T-shirt pulled tight over his chest. He smiled. 'No, ma'am.'

With the fire department right across the street and Cal obviously being on shift instead of chasing wildfires, it was hard to avoid him for too long.

He looked at my face, then my hands, which were gripping the life from my steering wheel.

'Want to talk about it?'

I shook my head. 'I just had a bad night.'

'Fair enough.' He opened my door, and I frowned.

'I wasn't ready to go in yet.'

'That's why I'm taking you to the station. You can hang out, tell me what's going on, then I can walk you back across the street when you're ready.'

When I went to argue, he grabbed my hand, helping me out of my car, and began walking me toward the firehouse. It was then I realized that he hadn't asked. He'd simply told me what he expected, and I did it. Like a trained doll. Shit! It was the casualness in his voice that'd thrown me off.

He punched in a code at the side door and led me in, down a narrow hallway, and into a large room filled with recliners and a big screen TV. What shocked me more was that there was a smattering of firefighters sitting in the recliners.

One man was in the middle of telling a dirty joke when all heads turned toward me in unison, like they simultaneously sensed a shift in the testosterone level. As I stood there, my mouth snapped shut, and I was stared at like some animal at the zoo. Silence.

'Well, hello there,' one man said, getting up from the recliner and snapping the footrest back into place. He strutted toward me, his gaze never leaving mine. 'Cal bring you for a tour? Because I'd be happy to show you around.'

'Ease off, Mark,' Cal said. 'She didn't come for a tour. Just wanted to introduce you before we headed to my room.'

All the guys looked at me, then Cal, and their expression was clear. It was practically inked onto their foreheads: 'Oh, we know why she came, wink, wink.'

'Yes, I did,' I said quickly. 'I came for the tour.'

Cal frowned at me. He had brought me here to 'talk,' but I wasn't about to let his crew think I was one of those girls that just

31

came in and headed straight for his bedroom. Based on the looks Cal was getting, no one was buying his 'talking' plan anyway.

'Excellent!' Mark said. 'Do you want to start here in the living quarters or with the trucks?'

'If she wants the tour, *I'll* give it to her,' Cal said with annoyance in his voice. 'But, unlike some of you jackasses, I have manners.' He cleared his throat and faced me. 'Lana, this is Mark, we let him hang out here sometimes.'

'Hey! I'm a legit firefighter.'

'Whatever, probie,' one of the guys in a recliner said.

'Probie?' I asked.

'He's still on his probation period,' Cal clarified.

'Only for another three months,' Mark said with a flirty smile aimed my way.

'And that's Able, Rhett, and Dave.' Cal pointed at the three men quickly. They all stood to greet me.

'Nice to meet you,' I said. They all just nodded. This was awkward. Like they didn't know how to talk to a female or something. Funny, since I'd caught glimpses of them before. Once at the park barbeque a while back and then at the Halloween party. But I'd never interacted with any of them. Though Rhett was the most familiar.

God, I wished I had some of that Harper power right now. The guys were obviously casual and enjoying themselves before I showed up. The tension needed to break, and for some reason, I wanted them to like me. This was a big part of Cal's world, and he'd invited me in. Well, he'd grabbed my hand and pulled me in, but I didn't want to disappoint. I wanted to hold my own.

'I heard you guys telling jokes?' I asked.

They looked between each other like they'd been caught doing something wrong.

What was that joke Harper always told? Oh!

32

'I have a joke, if you'd like to hear it?'

The men took a step closer. Dave said, 'Hell, yeah, I want to hear it!'

Mark smiled and crossed his arms. 'Yep, let's hear it.'

I glanced at Cal, and he looked just as anxious to hear what I was about to say.

I licked my lips, found my courage, and told the only joke I knew. The same joke Harper told me when I first met her to break the ice.

'How do you find a blind man in a nudist colony?' I asked.

The guys exchanged looks, then shook their heads, not knowing.

I simply shrugged and said, 'It's not hard.'

The room erupted with laughter and heat hit my cheeks. Cal rested his hand on the small of my back, his thick chuckle made a different kind of warmth rise in me.

'That was awesome,' Mark said. With that, everyone seemed to loosen up.

'She's a keeper, Cal,' Dave called, falling back into a recliner, still laughing.

Cal's hand on my back just rubbed a little, and an encompassing feeling of belonging hit me. Cal had this all the time. This brotherhood. I could tell from the interactions and conversations between all the guys, it was clear they were family. Even when they were flicking each other crap. The whole room felt full and happy. Not a sterile, uncomfortable thing passed between any of them.

'I'm going to show Lana the trucks now,' Cal said, and led me toward the garage.

'Hey, come back anytime, Lana!' Dave called, and Mark said something similar.

I glanced at my feet and smiled as we made our way toward the smell of oil, rubber tires, and fresh air. Cal opened the door, and there, on a slab of massive concrete surrounded by four concrete walls, two of which had large roll up doors, were shiny fire trucks.

'So, did you really want to see these, or are you just stalling?' he asked.

The door shut behind us and we were alone. I wound through the space, touching the biggest truck. The metal was cold and smooth. I'd never been so close to one, and it was shocking how large and long they were.

'Stalling?' I said with the best, 'Why, whatever do you mean?' drawl. I wound around the truck, my fingertips gliding along the smooth exterior as I did.

'Yeah,' Cal said. 'Another word for avoiding.' He maneuvered me against the side of the truck, my back pressing into the rig. He placed a palm by my head, leaning, and effectively caging me in.

'I was avoiding having your friends think I was some random woman you were taking to your room.'

His head dropped a little more, his face getting right in line with mine. 'I wouldn't let them think that about you, especially because there's nothing random about you.'

When I met his gaze, it put our mouths a whisper apart, and my lungs stuttered.

'I just want to talk. You looked like you're having a hard day.'

'Yeah,' I admitted. 'It's been frustrating.'

He clasped my hand in his, and when I thought he'd kiss me, he pulled away, taking me with him.

'We'll save the tour for another time,' he said, taking me back into the hall, only this time, instead of going toward the living area, he took a sharp left and went down a narrow hall with doors on each side. Bedroom doors.

He opened the one on the end. It was a small room with light blue walls and built-in cabinets. The Murphy bed was pulled down and lined with white sheets, a simple blanket, and two pillows. Aside from a few pictures taped to the wall, there was little else. This space was obviously meant for just sleeping. It was quiet, but I could hear the low hum of music and guys chatting off in the distance. Though Cal wanted to talk, and honestly, I wanted to vent, I still didn't like the idea of being viewed as 'that girl' by his crew.

'Everyone is still in the living room, and didn't see us come back here,' he said, as if reading my mind. He sat me down on the bed, then took a seat next to me. 'And, by the way, I'm not looking for you to be a random woman. I'm looking to know you.'

'You already know the gist,' I said casually. 'So, this is your room?'

'When I'm on duty, yes. But my house is only a few blocks away.'

I nodded.

'Stop stalling and tell me what's going on.'

I frowned at him. 'Stop telling me what to do.'

All the easygoing charm left his face. 'Look, I know what happened while you were with Jack. I know about your step-brother and your family of assholes. I know that they used you, I know that they hurt you. In a lot of ways. So, yeah, I know *the gist*.' His voice was vicious on the last statement, and I sat there in shock. Not because I didn't think it was possible he'd gotten details throughout the whole mess last month, but because he seemed to know about all of it and wasn't dancing around the truth.

'I'm on your side, Lana. I'm not going to pretend that your safety and wellbeing doesn't matter to me, because it does. I'm also not going to pretend that I am naïve to your family, especially your step-brother. So, if something is going on and you're in danger—'

'I took care of it,' I whispered, glancing at my hands. God, he knew more than I'd thought. 'Did Jack tell you everything?'

My heart sank because Cal's face turned heavy with emotion. He nodded once.

Great. So, he knew about my past with Brock, knew how he hurt me. He knew about my dad using me to get to Jack, which led to Jack leaving me.

'Tell me what you "took care of" tonight,' he said softly, and ran his finger along my chin.

I swallowed hard and looked up at him. 'Brock was by my car, waiting there after I got out of my meeting with my advisor.'

Cal took a deep, angry breath.

'Please tell me that you kicked him in the nuts and ran back inside.'

'No. I just told him I wasn't afraid of him, and I wasn't going to play his game. He's just trying to freak me out so, I got in my car and left.' Although it worked, the more time I had to think about the encounter, the more terrified I was becoming.

There I sat, on Cal's bed, and all I could do was stare at the ceiling and wonder what the hell I was going to do. When this would end?

Cal's whole hand cupped the side of my face, and he got real close, his bent knees brushing mine. 'The next time that asshole comes near you, you turn around and get to where people are. If he's at your school again, you go back inside. Understand?'

'No,' I shook his hand away. It was the 'understand?' that got me. Jack would tell me something, then follow up with that one, simple word. 'No, I don't *understand* because I'm not some weak pathetic thing that is going to cower from him.'

'I'm not talking about you cowering or being weak, I'm talking about physics.'

'Physics?' My balloon of anger deflated a little.

'I don't doubt your strength, Lana. I know you can handle yourself.'

36

Those words stuck to that empty spot in my chest and heated it a bit. Cal thought I was strong? Thought I could handle myself? His praise and confidence in me was something foreign and . . . nice.

'But if you believe that, then why are you telling me to run next time?'

Cal raised a brow like I'd lost my mind. 'Ah, A) because that dipshit is capable of a lot of things and B) he outweighs you. All he has to do is find a reason to snap and throw his weight around enough to get you in a bad position.'

And I knew what kind of position that was. One that left me vulnerable in more ways than one.

'You're a fighter, Kitten.' He winked, but the playful side of him lasted only a second. 'But, again, it's physics. The person with the more mass usually wins.'

Cal was right, it wasn't something to risk. Because, if there was one thing I knew, Brock may be showing up just to mess with my mind, but if he got angry, all bets were off. His calm, cool facade could turn violent in a heartbeat, and being on the receiving end of that was not a place I wanted to be ever again.

'Okay,' I said softly. 'You're right. I'll go where people are next time.'

'And call me,' he amended.

'Why?'

He glanced down the front of himself with his hands open, like I should understand. 'Mass,' he said with a grin. 'I guarantee I outweigh him, and I have no problem throwing *my* weight around.'

He winked, and I smiled. How he did this, I didn't know. He walked the fine line of control and casual. Alpha and sensitive. He gave me credit, yet played the role of protector. He was so . . . easy. No mind games. No guessing what his motives were. He simply just told the truth, put it all out there.

Still, keeping reality in my mind was smart. He said he cared about my safety. He likely felt a responsibility toward me because of the kind of man he was – a fighter and protector. Taking that notion too far would only lead to feelings. Something I was trying to stay away from in general.

I took a deep breath and combed my fingers through my hair.

'You looked tired,' he said, tucking a stray lock behind my ear and running his thumb along my cheekbone beneath my eye.

'Thanks for noticing,' I grumbled.

'Aw, don't get sassy, you're still hot.'

I laughed. 'Gee, thanks.' But his lack of seriousness made the moment more bearable. 'I haven't been sleeping well. And my thesis takes a lot of time, and I just found out tonight that there's more that I need to do. Not that I mind, it's actually a great idea my advisor came up with. I just don't know who, or where to really start.'

He whistled a low breath. 'Sorry, Kitten, I'm going to need some nouns to follow you here. What is it you need to do and who and where and . . . what?'

I laughed and Cal just smiled. Yeah, I suppose my conversational skills were coming out in less than complete thoughts or sentences. Still, he sat there, listening intently, those blue eyes soft with patience.

'I have to interview a local business owner. Shadow them even, and see how they run their company. It will help round out my project.'

'Wow,' he said.

I nodded. 'I just . . .'

'Don't know where to start?'

'Yeah.'

'What about starting with the interview?' I was about to tell him that yes, that's the perfect place to start, but the only two people I knew to interview were not going to happen. But then he added, 'My aunt is a small business owner here in Golden. It's a cleaning service, but she's pretty successful. I can set up an introduction if you'd like?'

My eyes went wide. 'Really? You'd do that?' So much hope lined my voice that even I could hear it. It was a win. Something Cal seemed to be able to deliver on. I wouldn't have to go into Denver and call around to get on someone's schedule. All because Cal was willing to help.

He smiled like his day had just changed, and his blue gaze went a little deeper as it focused on me.

'Yeah, of course I would.' His voice was low and soft and made shivers break out over my spine.

'You've just made my life so much easier,' I said, before I could think better of it.

'I'm glad. Now I have something serious to ask you.' He leaned in so close that his nose almost brushed mine. My breathing stalled and he grinned, stopping short of actually touching me. 'You ever going to admit how much you like kissing me?'

My lips parted thinking about just that. 'I ah . . . admit that it's complicated.'

'No, it's not.' He leaned closer. 'You like it.'

'I may.'

He raised a brow. 'May?' I shrugged a shoulder, and a playful growl escaped his throat. 'Sounds kind of like a challenge.'

Again, I shrugged a shoulder, but didn't get too far with that because his mouth was on mine in record time, kissing me like he would drink every last word, breath, and thought away. Leaving me with nothing to focus on, but him.

And I welcomed it.

Reaching to tunnel my hands in his hair, I stopped short.

Did that count as reaching out?

39

Before I could decide, he took another long draw from my mouth, like a man seeking his last taste of water. Decision made, gripping his hair didn't count as reaching out, it counted as holding on. Totally fine. So I did just that. I wove my fingers in his hair and kissed him back.

Plunging my tongue deep, I met his over and over, like I couldn't get enough. Because I couldn't. Every emotion I'd been carrying was seeping from my skin, and I couldn't fight it. So, I stopped fighting and gripped Cal's hair tighter. Kissed harder.

He cupped my hips and, in one easy slide, lifted me to straddle his lap like I weighed nothing, never breaking away from my mouth. I wanted more of him and less of the feelings that had been dark and carving a hollow place in my chest. For the moment, he filled that space. He was the warmth in the cold, and gave just a tiny glimpse of light against the darkness.

Every nerve I had snapped, and I clung to the feeling of him surrounding me. I was desperate for more. Desperate to know what it meant to be seen, touched, by this man.

'Do you think this is what we'd have done?' I said against his lips, breaking away just enough to yank his shirt over his head. I instantly started biting along his neck. 'After the night we met?' I kissed down his throat to his hard chest. The tattoo that marred his entire bicep snaked around his shoulder and covered the right side of his chest. It was amazing. The ink came alive as he moved, and I traced it with my tongue. 'Would we have come back in here and done this?' I sucked his nipple, and he hissed.

'We would have done a lot more than this,' he rasped, and unsnapped my jeans, tugging them open enough to slide his hand in.

I moaned with his palm pressed against my clit.

'Show me,' I said, fully in control, and no longer willing to be the scared girl I once was.

With one hand in my pants, his other cupped my neck and forced me to meet his gaze. We were both breathing hard, but an icy blaze lit his eyes.

'Who are you with right now?' he asked, his fingers, feather-light and slowly sliding back and forth with the barest touch, gently teasing me higher.

'You,' I replied instantly. I was with Cal. Strong, hard, casual Cal. And I wanted him. All of him. I was tired of drowning in the memories of my past, and that now included Jack. Bad idea or not, in that moment, I felt alive. Felt like I had a say in my world, all while feeling not so alone.

'Say my name.'

I realized then that this was important. That his name was a declaration that I was moving. Maybe not moving on, but moving in his direction.

'Cal,' I whispered.

A short grin split his face as he plunged his middle finger inside me. I gasped and gripped his shoulders. Again, simply to hold on, not to reach out.

With his palm against my clit and his finger deep inside me, I began to rock in his lap, fucking his finger the way I would his cock.

He kept a tight hold of me, letting me move how I wanted, but keeping me close. His muscles bulged and flexed because he leaned back just a little, causing his abs to strain and stand up like hunks of rock beneath tan skin.

He was like someone from myth. A descendant of Hercules himself. And I gave myself over to his power and strength. But I wielded my own power with my movements, keeping my pace and my control.

'Jesus, you feel amazing,' he said, and kissed down my throat to the neckline of my shirt. He bit the material and growled. 'Help me out, Kitten. My hands are busy.'

41

I yanked down my top and bra and wedged it beneath my breasts. The sounds of fabric ripping scratched my ears, but I didn't care.

He didn't say a word, just sucked my nipple into his mouth and pulled.

'Ah, God . . . yes.' I gripped him tighter, my fingernails digging into his skin, and I continued to ride his hand. My orgasm was just around the corner. He licked my breasts and my neglected skin sparked, like fire spreading over dry bark. The flames shot up from my core to my neck, burning me in the best way.

I wanted to feel him. Not reach, feel, I reminded myself.

I ran my hands down his stomach, those cut abdominal muscles turning me on even more.

'Mmmm,' he groaned, and sucked my other nipple into his mouth. My inner walls spasmed once, already on the brink. 'You're close, I can feel it,' he said, moving his palm in a circular motion, lighting up every nerve I had, and taking the fire to new heights. 'This tight, wet pussy is going to come all over my hand,' he rasped, and his words pricked my hairline with a fresh dose of lust. 'Let me feel it, Kitten. You wanted to know what it would have been like? I want to feel you writhe on my hand.'

I was helpless but to do just that. Because he held me tight, gently biting my nipple, and I shot over the edge like a rocket into pleasure. My whole body shuddered and came, just like Cal wanted, around his masterful hand. All the while, he gripped me tight and kept my head from lolling back in bliss.

With a deep breath, my eyes opened to find him staring at me. I realized then that this moment was intimate on a level I hadn't intended it to be. He'd just watched me come, and somehow, I'd gotten lost.

With shaky breaths, I moved to stand, his hand slipping from me and out of my pants. I buttoned my jeans quickly, and

42

adjusted my shirt so I was covered. But there was no hiding what had just happened. My emotions had gotten the better of me.

Cal sat forward, his eyes never leaving mine, and rested his elbows on his knees. All those muscles rippling, that tattoo flashing in the low light, and eyes blazing with intent.

He was beautiful.

'Cal, I'm sorry, but—'

'Nope,' he said quickly. 'I don't want to hear anything about being sorry. If that's the line you're thinking, then it would be better for you to just go.'

My mouth dropped. How had that happened? How had I gone from anger, to bliss, to brushed off in moments?

'I'm not doing this again. I'm not going to play mind games,' I said.

'Good, because I'm not either. And there is no *again*, when it comes to me. This is our first time, not our last, and not a repeat.' His expression was hard, and I knew what he meant. He wasn't Jack. Therefore, he was right, there was no *again* since there was no *before*. 'I want you. And if that means cleaning up his mess, I'll do it. But don't mistake my acknowledgment of reality for an invitation of your guilt.'

His words hit me harder than a strike to the face. 'This isn't easy,' I snapped. 'I'm still dealing with having my world fall apart and a man walk off with half my heart like I was nothing to him, while I stand here trying to pick up the pieces.'

'I know it's not easy. But everything you do, and everything you feel, is on you now. Own it. Don't be sorry for it.'

Rage and sadness speared my gut like a sharp knife. He was right. And it hurt. Truth did that sometimes. If I wanted to be strong, to be my own person and try to get past the last few months of my life, then I had to own it.

It didn't make it any less hard though.

'I'll call my aunt and set up a meeting,' he said, like he hadn't just been kissing me. 'As far as you and I go, if you want to run, fine, I can deal with that. But come find me when you're done hiding.'

44

Chapter 4

'How did the meeting with your advisor go?' Harper asked, as I walked through the front door.

'Fine,' I said, and locked the door behind me, the 'beep-beep' sounding right after from the alarm had turned into a comforting noise. The small reminder I needed that no one, not even Brock with his creepy stalking, could hurt me in here. I was in control. I had taken it back.

That was . . . until a few minutes ago when I walked out of the fire station.

'Just fine?' Harper asked, looking me over. 'You have sex hair.' Her eyes went wide. 'Please don't tell me you're screwing the professor?'

I rolled my eyes. 'She's a woman, and no.' I ran my fingers through my hair. 'It's just a little messy.'

Harper wasn't buying it. Especially since I had avoided her questioning glares since she'd crawled through the door yesterday with her own case of sex hair. I'd tried to ask her about the Viking, she asked me about my ride home with Cal, we both gave minimal information and neglected the real issues.

'Uh-huh, so how is Cal?' she asked. But before I could change the topic, she finished with, 'I saw you walking over to the station with him. Is that where the sex hair came from?'

'We didn't have sex,' I sat on the chair in the living room and pulled my knees to my chest.

'Maybe you should have.'

I frowned at my best friend. 'I thought you didn't even like him? At one point, you told me that he wasn't the right kind of guy for me.'

'That was at one point, not the point you're at now. I've watched you mope around here for weeks, and when you're with Cal is the only time you seem to smile. So if that overgrown fire chaser is what gets you hot and happy, then I say go for it.'

I shook my head and let out a long, long breath. 'I don't have the brain power for this tonight.'

'Still not sleeping?' Harper asked.

'No, not really.'

'Stress will do that.'

Yeah, stress. Or maybe it was the pit of despair in my gut that wouldn't go away and just turned into different shades of anger.

I didn't tell Harper about Brock. No need, since I had handled it. Whatever she saw on my face made her brows furrow, though, and she sat forward on the couch and looked at me. 'Why don't you come with me to my parents' house for Thanksgiving?'

I shook my head. It wasn't the first mention of this, but with Harper leaving the state in a few days, I appreciated her attempt to help.

'I can't,' I told her. 'But thank you so much for offering.'

I had my thesis to focus on, and Harper was set to stay for a few weeks. Plus, I didn't do well in family situations, typically, since I didn't really have a standard one growing up.

'Well, what are you going to do?'

'About what?' I asked.

'About Cal.'

Great, we were back on this. 'There's not much to do.'

'Oh, I disagree. There's plenty to *do*.' She winked.

'Seriously?'

'What?' she shrugged. 'The guy is a pain in the ass, but he's hot, and he likes you. He's been nice to you, despite his best friend being a dick.'

'Jack's not a dick.'

Harper raised a brow. I didn't like saying his name. Didn't like talking about him. Because I couldn't say anything negative out loud. Yes, Jack had a plan from the start, but he had also believed me when I'd told him that Brock had raped me when I was young. Despite my misguided attempt to fix things, Jack had still left believing me. Which was something. I loved him. Had loved him. Maybe a part of me always would. But it didn't change anything.

'It's time to move on,' Harper said, like she had been saying for weeks. I thought of Cal's advice.

'What if I just move instead?'

'What the hell does that mean?' Harper asked.

'I don't know. Take baby steps.'

'Honey, you need to take leaps and bounds away from Jack, his memory, and your family.' Harper was so good at telling me what my problem was and what I should do, though she wasn't exactly wrong. It came from a good place. I just processed differently than she did.

'Look, I think that this moment in your life is a big one. You can either let the past crush you, or rise above it.'

I thought about what I'd just done with Cal. How his body felt against mine. His hands on me, in me. I shuddered at the thought, and what surprised me was that I wanted more. More of his touch. More of the kind of dominance he brought to the table. Yes, there were similarities between him and Jack, but wild differences too. Cal told me what he wanted, then let me respond how I chose. It was my choice, my control, my say.

There was something heady about that.

I wanted more.

I wanted to feel that kind of lost empowerment again. Wanted to touch all his strength and make it my own by exercising my will, my wants, over him. It hit me just then:

He let me be angry.

He knew he was cleaning up Jack's mess, and still took the job anyway and let me do what I needed to do. And just held me tight.

Shit. I was in trouble. Because any kind of attachment to another man, especially Cal, was not something my emotional system could handle. My body was screaming for more, maybe even my mind, but my heart? Bad. Bad, bad idea.

My phone beeped with a text. I reached behind me to the small table and grabbed it.

Cal: My Aunt is free Thursday if you'd like to meet around lunchtime. I can take you.

My heart took a slow free fall. He set this up. Was helping me. Asking for nothing in return. Yet the look in his eyes when I left tonight was serious. I could run, but he wouldn't let me hide. Which was what I wanted to do. Needed to do before things got even more complicated, and more feelings got involved.

My phone pinged again.

Cal: It's just a simple lunch, Kitten. Don't think yourself out of an easy win.

Cal was right. This lunch was something I needed, and I needed a win. I just needed to be careful and maintain a friend-ship level barrier. Somehow, I'd figure out how to do that with Cal. Though friends didn't typically stick their hands down your pants. But I had to make whatever was happening between us stop, though everything in me was cursing the thought. Because he felt good. So damn good. But that kind of good led down a path I didn't want to be on again. It led to needy. Led to vulnerability. Led to loss.

Friends. I could keep Cal as a friend.

Me: Thursday is great. I'll be ready at noon. Thank you.

There. Simple. To the point. I'd have this interview, revise my thesis proposal, and that would be it.

Yet, somehow, nothing seemed that simple.

I sat in Cal's truck as he turned off Main Street and wove a few miles around a residential area. Golden wasn't too big, which was largely appealing to me.

The sun was shining bright, burning off last night's inch of fluffy snow that had fallen. The sound of the truck tires spinning along wet pavement kicked up the smell of afternoon dew and autumn. I loved my town. Every once in a while, when I remembered to stop and really appreciate the calmness, I found myself enjoying the still light. It was amazing what a little sunshine could get you excited for.

However, the thing I wasn't overly excited about was Cal's silent treatment. He just stared straight ahead, saying nothing. Which made looking at his mouth worse, since I knew how it moved. And that was something I was trying not to focus on, yet the only image my brain churned out.

'How have your last few days been?' I asked. He hadn't reached out since the text letting me know his aunt would meet with me, which was where we were going now.

'Pretty good. Had three on and now four off, so can't complain. Been quieter now that we're out of summer fire season.'

'No more running after wild fires?' I asked.

'Not for a while.'

The conversation was tight, forced. His hand on the steering wheel looked casual, but the white in his knuckles showed he was gripping it pretty hard. Was he upset from the other night?

Was I upset?

I wasn't exactly beaming sunshine, but I had no idea what to say or where to go. Keeping things casual with Cal was a better idea than starting any kind of relationship with him. Physical or otherwise. Mostly because I wasn't a woman who separated physical and emotional easily, and also because I loved being touched and taken over. I also loved getting a taste of power. Which was exactly what I'd gotten the other night with Cal.

The few times I'd taken over in the bedroom with Jack, I'd either gotten spanked, which I actually liked, or he 'allowed' me to take over first and only in small, brief ways. Jack needed his control and I'd understood, enjoyed everything we did. But I was not with Jack anymore.

Nope. Cal was in casual in jeans and a long-sleeved black shirt that clung to his muscles and made my mouth water like a dehydrated nympho. Because all I could think about was touching those muscles again. Feeling them.

My one saving grace was that we hadn't crossed a line that we couldn't cross back from. At least I hoped not. If I could figure out how to maintain 'friend status' and not want to throw myself into his arms, maybe I could continue down this path of self-preservation.

'Thinking about something over there,' he said, glancing at me. I was working my bottom lip and realized I was frowning in his direction. Whoops.

'I was just thinking about a conversation I had with Harper.'

He nodded. But didn't ask for more. Maybe because I got irritated the last time he tried and I'd compared his verbiage to Jack's? Suddenly, I felt shitty about that. I felt shitty about a lot of things. And, for whatever reason, I continued as if he'd asked for more detail anyway.

'She was telling me for the thousandth time that I need to really move on from both Jack and my family.'

'Has your step-brother caused any more problems since showing up at your school?' he asked quickly.

'No. And I'm not scared of him.' Not in the way I use to be at least. He couldn't impact my world if I didn't let him. 'It's hard letting go of certain things, even when the good moments you're holding on to aren't worth the pain they cause now.'

'Jack,' Cal said, like that one word summed up my entire problem.

I shook my head. 'I was talking about my dad.'

Cal sent me a sidelong glance, then focused back at the road. It was like he was asking me to go on without actually saying it. He already knew the worst, may as well spill the rest.

'I'd held on to this idea that my dad and I would be close again. I know now it won't happen. He's a different man. Even I'm different. But when everything hit, it hit at once. I really thought, one day, I'd work for him, we'd be a family and, yeah ... Jack was in my future thoughts too.' I shook my head and moved past that quickly. 'But all of that was gone in the matter of one afternoon.'

Cal nodded. 'And you were left having to readjust and re-plan a life you never thought you'd have to.'

'Yeah, that's exactly it.' I'd never thought outside the box I was living in. Crippled by fear and desperate to be a staple in my father's world had been my path. Then Jack came along and things changed. I became stronger, held more self-worth. Then my father showed his true colors, and I ended up losing Jack and everything I'd ever thought I could have.

Everything I once wanted.

Cal turned down one more street and came up on a charming little blue house with white shutters. He put the truck in park and faced me.

'Shit happens that you can't control,' Cal said, and my eyes shot wide. No sugarcoating, no tiptoeing, he just came right out with what was on his mind. 'But the only thing you can do is hold on to what you have left and do whatever you have to do to make your life bearable. If you're lucky, you'll find something that even makes it enjoyable.' His gaze seared mine and I forgot how to breathe. He spoke as if he knew what loss felt like.

'Like school,' he finished quickly.

'What?'

'School is important to you. Something that you worked hard for. Hold on to that, if nothing else.'

He got out of his truck, leaving me with my mouth parted and my brows drawn. He came around to open my door and help me out, and walked me up to the little house not saying another word.

He knocked once, then opened the door.

'Aunt Bea?' Cal called.

A cheery voice sounded from inside, followed by the scuttle of feet coming toward us as Cal led me into the kitchen.

'There's my sweet boy.' A short, round woman with cropped graying hair and bright eyes entered the open kitchen from another room. Her arms were wide as she closed in on Cal. He hugged her tight, gave a bear growl, and she laughed. Cupping his elbows, she looked at him. 'You staying safe? Eating alright? You look scrawny.'

Cal looked scrawny? Holy crap, I didn't want to know what beefy looked like then.

'I'm good,' Cal said, and put his arm around her and faced me.

'Aunt Bea, this is Lana Case, a friend of mine. Lana this is my amazingly wonderful Aunt Beatrice.'

She laughed and swatted him on the chest, then turned her attention to me.

'It's so nice to meet you, Lana.' She came at me with those wide arms open again and hugged me. The action was so surprising that it almost toppled me over. But she smelled like sugar cookies, and I realized that it had been a long time since any kind of mother figure had hugged me.

'Come, sit at the table. Cal said you have some questions for a project?'

'Yes, thank you,' I said.

Cal sat across the little circular table from me, while Bea grabbed a tray from the kitchen counter. The white and blue checkered linoleum squeaked beneath her orthopedic shoes as she came back with cookies. That explained the smell. But I was pretty sure she likely smelled like sugar and happiness all the time. It just radiated from her.

She set the treats in the middle of the table and urged us both to take one. I did. 'Thank you, this is really nice.'

'Of course,' she said, and sat next to me. 'When Callum said he was bringing a girl over, I was so excited.' She leaned in and with a loud whisper said, 'He's never brought one home before.'

I looked at Cal, and the big man was blushing. 'This is for her school project,' Cal clarified. Suddenly, I felt like we were a couple of high schoolers and Bea's sweet demeanor had us both a little red in the face.

'Yes, yes,' she said, waving a hand.

I pulled out my laptop and opened a blank page to take notes. I explained the basics of what I was doing, outlining what I needed for my proposal. She nodded, and it was no hard feat to get her chatting.

'Well, I started my cleaning business right after I got Callum, about twenty-five years ago. I must say that, even during the recession, we've still kept our head above water, and I credit that to stellar customer service and having a personal touch that a lot of big cities can't match.'

I nodded and typed. She answered my questions, giving me good information. Then she turned the questions back on me.

'So tell me, what is it you are trying to do with this project?'

'I'm trying to get my masters' degree.'

'Oh, how nice!' she said. 'And you want to be a business owner?'

I went to answer, then stopped for a moment. I'd hatched the grand plan of me working for my father and becoming a financial analyst a long time ago. But things had changed.

'Honestly, I've never considered owning my own business. I've always wanted to be a part of a business, though. Help people succeed and make smart choices with their money and investing.'

'That sounds great,' Bea said. 'A lot of people need help being smart with their money.' She winked at me. 'I may have you take over my books!'

I was pretty sure she was kidding, but her jolly demeanor paired with a serious expression made me pause.

Thankfully, I didn't have to come up with a response because she turned to Cal and said, 'This girl is a smart one,' Bea snapped her fingers to her nephew, then pointed at me as if he wasn't sitting right there and knew who she was talking about. Still, I was blushing a little more. I'd never been praised really or called smart. With my dad, it was how I was lacking, how I needed to do more to keep up with Brock.

'She's very smart,' Cal agreed.

And the blush went to DEFCON-Rudolph-Red.

'I want to hear more about you, Lana. How does your project

relate to my cleaning business, and do you like cranberry sauce?' she asked, resting her hand on her cheek and looking at me with so much delight I thought she was seeing some magical fairy instead of a regular human.

Those were two wildly different questions, but she just waited, like they went together easily. So I tackled the first question.

'I'm actually going to apply my thesis to your business and experience and do a mock up analysis.'

'Oh! Sounds fun. What does that mean?'

'It's just some possible financial options and strategies for investments based on your hypothetical needs and interests. Then I present that to my advisor.'

'And then your advisor gives you your masters'?'

'She has to approve it and take it to a thesis board.'

'Good Lord,' Bea said. 'I'm exhausted just listening to all these steps. You should be proud of yourself for going so far with this. It's really special, Lana. That's very impressive.'

I blinked rapidly because there was a weird sting that crept up behind my eyes suddenly.

I shrugged. 'It sounds more complicated than it is.'

'No, she's impressive,' Cal cut in, telling his aunt exactly what he thought. 'Dedicated and thoughtful and grounded.'

'Another word for boring,' I joked.

'Well, whatever the title is, you need more of Lana in your life,' Bea said to Cal. 'I've never been able to get this one to sit in one place for long. Always searching for something to terrify me.'

'Ah, here we go with the guilt,' Cal grumbled.

'Not guilt. I just would like you to live a long and happy life ... preferably not tossing yourself into a fire like damn pizza.'

Aunt Bea was brassy, and I could see where she and Cal were similar. She was kind and sweet, but didn't pause at telling you what she thought. I thought about the place Cal took me to on

Halloween. The fire he almost didn't make it out of. Poor Bea must have been worried. In Cal's line of work, I couldn't imagine that was his only brush with death or injury.

'I tried to get him to be one of those nice gentlemen that go around town in those little cars and makes sure all the fire zones are clear,' Bea continued.

'That's parking patrol,' Cal said with a sigh, like he'd heard this a million times before.

'It's safe, and you still work with fire of sorts.'

'That's not the same thing at all.' But instead of arguing further, he stood, and kissed the top of her head. 'I'll let you two finish up here. I'm going to turn on the game in the living room.' With a glance at me, Cal walked into the other room and out of sight.

Bea sighed. 'He's such a good boy. Stubborn. I worry, and I know it bothers him.'

'I don't think it bothers him,' I said. 'I can tell why Cal is so protective of the people he cares about. He gets that from you.'

She smiled, and I felt like maybe I'd helped. It was a nice feeling. Probably even nicer to have someone support and care about you so much that they worried for your wellbeing. Cal was lucky to have this woman in his life. Which made me think of something she'd mentioned earlier.

'You'd said that you got Cal twenty-five years ago?'

She glanced down, and something very painful lit her face. 'Yes. When his mother died, my sister, I got custody.'

'Oh, I'm so sorry.'

'Thank you, honey. It was hard. I know I fuss over him more than I should, but I just . . . ' she glanced at where Cal had just been. 'There's a part of him that's shut down, even as a child, and I've never been able to reach it.'

My heart ached for them both. I wanted to tell her not to

56

worry so much. That Cal was wonderful. Casual and funny and didn't seem like anything really affected him.

Maybe that was what she was talking about, though. Not much seemed to rock Cal's casual demeanor. Yet, this morning was the most tense I'd ever seen him.

'Came in for a cookie,' Cal said, walking back into the kitchen. He stopped to look at me, then Bea, obviously sensing the conversation had changed. 'You done?'

I nodded. 'I think I have everything I need.' I powered down and packed up. Bea stood and hugged me tight. Though we'd just met, her hugs were like candy. I wanted just a few more because they left a sense of happiness behind. 'Thank you so much.'

'Anytime, honey,' she said. 'Wait!' Her voice screeched with so much power it made me physically halt. 'You never said if you like cranberry sauce?'

'Oh.' Right, that question. I had avoided it because, in all honesty, the one time I remember even being near cranberry sauce was back when my parents were together. My mother had opened the can and laid it on the plate and started cutting slices. But I never tried it. I must have been really young, because it was the only memory I could pull up of both my parents in the same room.

'I can't remember ever having it,' I finally admitted.

Bea looked like I'd just uttered an unholy prayer to the devil himself.

'Well, that is going to have to change,' she said with determination.

'My aunt's cranberry sauce is the best in the state,' Cal whispered.

'Best in a couple states,' she mumbled. 'But please come back. Whether he brings you or not. You're always welcome.'

'Thank you, that's really nice.' And something I wish I could take her up on, because based on my earlier plan of attempting to keep it casual with Cal, the warmth I felt from him, and now his aunt, were filling my chest with an emotion I hadn't felt for a while.

Longing.

To be a part of a family. A real family that loved and supported one another.

They aren't my family, I reminded myself quickly. I was coveting something that wasn't mine to covet. But, if I were honest, I wanted this moment to last just a bit longer. To feel like these walls somehow shielded me from the outside and all the mess that came with it.

'Love you,' Cal said to his aunt and hugged her goodbye.

A muffled, 'Love you too, kiddo,' came from her, and it made my eyes water a little. What it must be like to have someone care so deeply for you. A parent. She may not have given birth to Cal, but she loved him unconditionally, that much was so obvious it was almost a foreign concept. Because the only experiences I'd had seemed to always come with conditions.

Cal picked up my bag, carrying it for me, and with a hand on the small of my back, led me out the front door and to his truck. Every move had thought and grace in it. Like a protector. As if this was the way he was meant to move.

Once we were on the road, heading back toward my place, I turned in my seat and faced him.

'Thank you so much. Your aunt is really wonderful.'

'Yeah, she is.'

'So, she really wanted you to be on parking patrol, huh?'

'When I told her I wanted to go into training for the fire squad, she countered with that. It never stuck.'

'I can't see you fitting into one of those little cars anyway.'

'Yeah, that was the deal breaker.'

'She obviously cares, though.'

'I know. But she also knows that I need a certain level of . . .'

'Adrenaline?' I finished for him.

He looked at me. 'Something like that.' His eyes were back on the road. There was more to Cal, more to this conversation and his needs than I was aware of. But, clearly, I wasn't going to get more details. Because now wasn't the time, and that kind of connection was something that I was trying to avoid . . . right?

My mind seemed to have other ideas, and wanted to know more, though.

'I'm sorry to hear about your mom—'

'Did you always want to go into finance?' he asked, cutting me off. I paused, but went with his new direction. A different kind of tension was radiating from him. Riding in his truck, talking about his deceased mother probably wasn't high on the list of things he wanted to do. Especially since I didn't think I was high on his list of people he was overly happy with at the moment.

'Kind of. I like having a plan, organization, numbers and strategy, and—'

'Control?'

'Yeah, I suppose so.'

He nodded. 'Well, you're very good at what you do.'

'How could you possibly know?' I didn't mean for that to sound bitchy. I was legitimately curious because I didn't even know if I was good at it.

He didn't miss a beat, though. That blue gaze landed on me. 'Because of the way you think.'

'What way is that?'

He was back to looking out the window, but smiled. 'With logic and passion.'

I swallowed hard. His words clicking into place and hitting

59

what I was as a person, down to my soul. Logic and passion —
always at odds. Never a balance. Always one overtaking the other.
For a long time, it was logic. Trying to deal with Brock, what he'd
done to me and the past. I'd find excuses and logic in my life to
explain away details. I needed that to function.

Then, Jack and Cal came along and, suddenly, passion won
out. Kissing Jack, then Cal the next week? Both instances were
lapses in judgment and operated purely on emotion.

Which was why I was in the mess I was in now.

'I don't know if that does me any favors,' I admitted.

'I think it does. It means that you can be cautious, yet still take
a risk when needed. Which is good, since you want to deal with
people's money.'

Right. That. That was what we were talking about. Though the
look in his eyes made me think there was way more in the under-
tone of this conversation than just my critical thinking skills in
the workplace.

'Cautious and risky can be exhausting,' I said lowly.

'I'm sure it is, Kitten.' My ears perked a little when he called
me that. Usually, it came out at least once in our conversations,
and it hadn't today until just now. 'Which is why I choose just
risky.'

'No kidding.' He was the poster boy for testosterone and
adrenaline-chasing alpha awesomeness. 'Did you always want to
be a firefighter?'

'No, I wanted to be a super hero until I was eighteen.'

I laughed, so did he. It was nice chatting like this. At least we
were getting out of the lull that started the day. We pulled up to
my house, and he faced me.

'When is the next meeting with your advisor?' he asked.

'I meet with her every Monday. So, I have a few days to rewrite
my draft. Your aunt really helped.'

'Good to hear,' he said. 'I'm interested in hearing how it goes.'

'Okay. Maybe I can give you a call or something Monday and catch up?'

'You know where to find me.'

And there it was. The reminder of how we left things, rather, how I'd walked out on things a few nights ago. He'd told me his stance, and watched me leave. He gave me the control to seek him out instead of the other way around.

'Thank you again,' I said, and climbed out of his truck. With my bag and a long weekend of work ahead of me, I wondered if it would be enough to get Cal out of my mind.

Chapter 5

Standing on the other side of Erica's desk, I watched my advisor flip through my revised thesis proposal. It had taken me all weekend, but implementing Bea's business as the model filled out the project.

Erica scanned another page, reading quietly.

I started biting my thumbnail.

Finally, she tugged her glasses off. 'This is great. Exactly what I was thinking, and the way you tied your project with a real business will really impress the board.'

'Really!'

'Yes. I think I'm ready to sign off on it.'

I wanted to hug her. Instead, I tried not to jump up and down. 'Thank you so much.'

She seemed to read my body language because she stood up and hugged me. 'Really, well done. Just give me a couple days to really read it over, and then we'll take it to the board.'

'Okay, great.'

I tugged my bag onto my shoulder and she leaned against her desk. 'So, before you go, how's life going?'

'Life is going pretty well,' I said. But what was awesome was that I meant it.

'That's great. Did you get that waiter's number? Because you seem happier.'

'No, not the waiter . . .'

Her eyes got wide. 'Why, Lana Case, are you being social?'

Heat hit my cheeks. 'A little.'

'Good! Keep it up! Sorry we had to meet in my office this week, but next week I say we try the tapas place right across the street.'

'Sounds great.'

After another wide smile, I walked from her office and out into the parking lot. It felt good to be succeeding at something. Something I controlled. Something that was just mine and I could be proud of—

'Shit,' I muttered when I saw Brock pull into the parking lot. What the hell was his problem? Did he make it a ritual to wait for me after class just to annoy me? I wanted to continue to my car, but thought about what Cal had said. If Brock was crazy enough to mess with me just to try to inspire fear, it wasn't worth taking on a potentially dangerous situation.

I turned, hustled back inside, and headed straight for Erica's office.

'Lana?' she asked, surprised when I just bolted in. 'Are you alright?'

'Yes, sorry I just got spooked walking in the parking lot.' I didn't want to say that my step-brother was trying to make my life miserable, but close enough.

'This time of year, the campus seems to get darker and more desolate even earlier than usual. I was getting ready to leave too, we can walk out together.'

'I'd appreciate that.'

'Let me just pack up here,' she said, putting my proposal and her laptop in her bag, 'And I'm just waiting for—'

'Hey, babe,' a voice said from the doorway. The same voice that plagued my nightmares. I turned and saw Brock.

'Hi!' Erica said, and hustled over to kiss him. My eyes shot wide. 'Lana, this is my fiancé, Brock VanBuren.'

No. No, this wasn't happening.

'Lana is scared to walk to her car,' Erica said to him, putting a hand on his chest. 'So, I told her we could walk her?'

'Of course we can,' Brock said with a smile, throwing his arm around Erica.

I opened my mouth to say something. Something along the lines of 'Run!' or 'Please, God, wake me up from this nightmare.' But Brock beat me to it.

'And no need for an introduction, babe,' he said to Erica. 'Lana here is family. Right, sis?'

I choked on the instant bile that rose in my throat. But Erica seemed just as taken aback as I was.

'Oh, I didn't know.' She glanced between Brock and me.

'It's a fun surprise. I knew Lana went to school here, but didn't know she had the best professor on campus,' he said, and kissed her quickly. I wanted to hurl. He was so smooth and easy to believe.

It was obvious that Erica did. Her face was flushed with excitement, and I could see the adoration in her expression when he tightened his arms around her and cradled her into his side. My professor – my friend – was in love. With my rapist.

I wanted to keel over.

'Step-sister,' I finally said. The only words that made sense and I could muster to come out of my shocked mouth. Both Brock and Erica frowned at me like I'd just spoken a different language. I gathered myself quickly. 'I'm his *step*-sister. And, yes, this is quite a surprise.'

Erica snuggled deeper into Brock, her arm lovingly slid around him, connecting them as a single unit. Reminding me, once again, when it came to my family, it was me standing against them. Alone.

'Well, that explains why I didn't know by your last name. Good thing he showed up. You ready to go to your car?' she asked.

I wanted to tell her, no, I didn't want to go anywhere with him, then steal her away and tell her everything. Call him out on the horrible person he was. On what he did to me. To my family. But my mouth wouldn't move. My feet just carried me like a zombie to my car, following behind Brock and Erica, as my mind tried to process how the one area in my life I was proud of, thought I had control of, was now within Brock's clutches.

'Great job again on the proposal,' Erica said, as I got into my car. 'Can't wait for our meeting next Monday.'

I felt sick. Monday was something I had been looking forward to, had been working all semester to achieve. Finally going to the board. Only now, getting that final write-off from Erica would mean inviting the one person I had worked so hard to exorcise from my life, back in.

'Erica, wait,' I said. 'I need to talk to you.'

She turned toward me, but Brock kept her close. 'Actually, we're heading to the airport,' Brock said, then turned his attention on Erica. 'We're already running late, babe.'

'Oh.' She checked her watch. 'Shoot! Yes, we are. I have a conference this week in Phoenix. So sorry, Lana, but let's talk Monday, okay?' She waved and hustled with Brock in the other direction.

'You drive safe now, sis,' Brock said with a wink, but his stare was cold and threatening. It was the first time I felt truly terrified of him in weeks. I started my car and sped off, wondering if this was what shock felt like. No, no I didn't need to wonder. I was pretty sure this was shock.

I parked in front of my house, but didn't go in.

I inhaled through my nose and exhaled out of my mouth, trying to take calming breaths. I could deal with this . . . I could deal with this . . .

All that strength I was trying to obtain was nowhere to be found. All the practice of beating back fear and anxiety wasn't helping. But I still tried. Tried to handle what had just happened. Tried to handle the fact that Brock was back in my life, despite my best efforts.

My eyes hurt from the strain of keeping back tears. Angry tears. All while trying not to hate myself for being damn near mute. Maybe I should have screamed? Tried harder to tell her? Yell if I had to. But I didn't. I watched her walk away with my sick step-brother.

I needed a sounding board. Needed to gather myself. Needed a plan.

I ran across the street toward the fire station. Little flecks of rain started coming down, the kind that carried a gust of wind with them and stung when they hit my face.

Ringing the bell, I crossed my arms tightly around myself and bounced on my toes. I waited and finally the door opened and it was Cal.

'What happened?' he asked instantly, concern knitting his brow. 'Are you okay?'

'No, I'm not okay . . . I need you.'

My heart was beating so fast I could feel it in my throat. I paced back and forth in Cal's room, clenching and unclenching my fists. But there was nothing to grab. Nothing to hold on to.

'I should have told her!' I said, continuing my strides along the walls of his room like a caged animal. 'I just stood there, horrified, while he smiled and kissed her, and I just . . . froze. How could I do that?'

'It's okay,' Cal said, and gently cupped my shoulders, halting my frantic back and forth movement.

'No, it's not okay. What if he hurts her?'

66

Cal looked down at me, his thumbs rubbing slowly on my skin, keeping eye contact. 'If he'd hurt her, you would have been able to tell.'

The idea made me shudder, but Cal was right. If Brock had shown her his true nature, Erica would have likely been some level of solemn, but she was all giddy and happy. Which meant she had no idea about the kind of man Brock really was.

'I should have said something,' I whispered.

'You were shocked, it happens. Don't give yourself a hard time about this. Now, you have time to think about how you want to handle this.'

'I want to tell her,' I said, knowing that I couldn't live with myself if I didn't.

'Okay,' he said with all the support in the world. 'Then let's figure out the best way to go about that. But first, I want you to take a deep breath.'

I huffed out. Not because I was frustrated with Cal, but because I hadn't been taking actual breaths. Just short puffs of air. One long inhale did help, so I took another. My body relaxed a little.

'At least I know why he's been on campus,' I whispered, hating the idea of Brock being with my sweet advisor. She was kind and smart, and he obviously had her blinded to the real monster that hid under the cultured manners and expensive clothes. But that was his strong suit. Making people buy into his charm and charisma.

'You said you meet with her every Monday. Why not talk to her then?'

'That's a week away.' And so much could happen in a week. Hell, someone's entire world could change forever in a single night.

'I know what you're thinking,' Cal said gently. 'But I don't think Brock will hurt her. It's not the same situation.'

'I know, but she deserves to know the kind of man he is. What he's capable of.' I patted his chest in rapid succession. An idea striking me. 'She's gone this week in Phoenix, maybe I could call the school and get her cell phone number! Or maybe I can figure out what hotel she's staying at.'

'Shhh, calm down, Kitten,' Cal's voice was the only thing calm happening right now. 'I know you want to tell her, and you should. But, like you said, she's gone this week, and even if the school gave you her number, which they won't, this isn't exactly an email or phone call kind of situation.'

He had a point. This was a big issue, and not something a quick call could cover. But I hated the idea of waiting. Still, I didn't have much choice.

'Okay, I want to talk to her face to face.' My brain went into overdrive of what I'd say. How could I say it? It's not like you could just walk up to someone and say, 'Hey, the guy you want to spend the rest of your life with is a monster, now, let me tell you why . . . ' Still, it was definitely an in-person chat, no matter how difficult.

'I think that's best,' Cal said.

Okay. Monday, one week, and I'll tell her. It would give me time to collect myself and think of how to approach this logically. Because the more the craziness of the moment cleared, the more I realized how difficult this was. For all she knew, Brock was wonderful. Her fiancé. The man she loved enough to spend the rest of her life with. And, in one moment, I was going to ruin all of that.

I knew what that felt like, to have your entire world ripped out from under you, and I realized I was going to tell her something truly awful.

'Okay,' I said on a heavy breath. 'Monday.'

He rubbed my arms. 'Good, now that you have a plan, I want to know if you are okay?'

'Yeah, I mean, he didn't do anything.'

'That's not what I mean. This is a big blow, you're worried about your advisor, but how do you feel?'

I looked at the ground and a cold chill pricked over my skin as I remembered his eyes on me. How he winked. How he looked so evil. How terror engulfed me. It was paralyzing. And I hated that he still had that power over me, even in the smallest way. Even for one moment.

Did Brock pick Erica *because* she was my advisor? Did he do this on purpose? It was too coincidental to think this was purely random. Brock always had a plan. He also had a hobby of evoking fear. But I didn't know for certain what his end game was, or what Erica had to do with it.

'Things are falling apart,' I whispered. School was my one sanctuary. My domain. My place of acceptance and success. And now Brock was, once again, there with all the baggage and drama and pain that came with him. There was nowhere left to hide.

Cal had warned me from the beginning about hiding, but I wasn't ready to be a part of the world right now. I wasn't ready to face the mess that was raining down. I'd been fighting a losing battle for a long time. Right when I thought I'd finally gained ground, I was pushed back. My body couldn't take anymore. Couldn't handle the weight of all the stress. I couldn't bear to lose one more thing.

I said the same thing I'd said to Cal the night I met him. 'I need a win.'

His face was like stone. Did he remember that first night? When we'd won a silly fireman's race, but it made my night, my week, seem better. It was a brief moment of easy happiness.

'I can't hide,' I admitted, and he nodded in agreement. 'But I don't want to be like this. I feel trapped in a bad situation and just want to ...'

'Run?' he asked.

'Right off the edge of the world.'

A devilish grin came over his face. 'I can help with that.'

'What?' I asked with curious shock.

'You want off the world?' He grabbed my hand and whistled loudly, calling out the other firefighters on duty, while walking me toward the garage where they kept the trucks. 'I can get you off the world, Kitten.'

Chapter 6

'So, you ready for this, Lana?' Dave asked, as he put big block things on each side of the wheels, 'stabilizing the truck.' I had met Cal's crew briefly before, but standing in the dark, with the big fire truck pulled out into the back lot while four men went to work on pulling out beams from secret compartments on the rig and securing it, I was getting to know both the crew and the details of how this massive machine worked better.

'Yeah, I am,' I answered, crossing my arms, warding off the cool night air. Thank goodness it had only sprinkled for a moment earlier. The sky was now clear and black with the stars like diamonds shining down.

'You know, Cal's been gabbing like a tween about you ever since you were here last.'

'Shut the fuck up, Dave,' Cal said, walking from the garage toward the truck, holding a fire jacket in his hand. Another thing I was learning quickly was that the guys seemed to enjoy giving each other a hard time. But they had a dynamic like a family. Cal had merely asked for some help, and they came running. Help for what, I wasn't clear on yet. But it had something to do with this massive fire truck that was both turned on and had a few guys standing by.

'You ready?' Cal asked and held up the heavy yellow jacket. I eyed it with question.

'Ready for what? You leading me into a fire?'

'No, way better. Put this on, it's cold.'

I slipped into his coat. It smelled fresh, as if it'd just been cleaned. And, like Cal, it was warm and instantly comforting. Sure, it dwarfed me, but I wasn't cold anymore.

'Now, smile!' Dave said, and snapped a photo on his camera phone.

'Oh!' I said, when the flash took me by surprise.

'Cal's throwing up the stick and taking a lady, gotta document this stuff for the scrapbook.'

'I'm sorry, I only understood half of that,' I said.

'We make scrapbooks,' Cal said in my ear. 'Well, Dave mostly does. He's our arts and crafts coordinator, aren't you, Davy?'

'No, I'm the Tickle Tuesday Ambassador. Rhett is in charge of the arts and crafts. He has those delicate hands and all.'

'I heard that!' Rhett called out from the other side of the truck.

'Good, maybe then you'll stop stealing my lotion!' Dave called back.

'Are you two arguing over lotion again?' Mark said, coming around to stand at the back of the truck. It appeared he was attempting to grow a mustache since I'd seen him last. 'Rhett needs it more than you do, Dave. That guy hasn't gotten laid in a while.'

'Will you shut up,' Rhett said, looking at me, then at Dave and Mark. 'There's a lady here.'

'*The lady* probably can tell you're not getting laid either. It's no secret.' Mark made a hand gesture that signified exactly what everyone thought Rhett to be doing with said lotion.

I tried not to laugh, but the way the guys were with each other was hilarious. Dave just slapped his buddy's back. 'It's okay, Rhett. You can keep the lotion.'

'Sharing is caring,' Mark finished.

'Jesus Christ,' Rhett muttered and walked off.

'Aw, poor guy,' I said. 'You embarrassed him.'

'This is nothing,' Cal said. 'Rhett may be stomping away, but he's already plotting revenge. Within the hour, he'll unleash some kind of hell on us. Probably take that lotion and spread it all over our pillows.'

'And you all are friends?'

'Best of,' Dave said. 'Don't worry, after you leave, we'll give Cal shit too for having you over again. But we're wearing our polite hats now.'

'Oh, boy,' I said with a small laugh. These guys were so laid back and funny it was hard not to get caught up in it.

'Throwing the stick is what we say when we take the ladder out,' Cal clarified part of Dave's earlier statement. He stepped up, one, two, three, big steps to get to the first level of the fire truck. He held a hand down, reaching for me.

I looked up at him, then at the big ladder that was currently resting happily horizontal on top of the truck.

'I'm going on that?' I asked.

'Nope, *we're* going on that.' He glanced at the ladder.

With a deep breath, I reached for the handle, put my foot in the first rung, and started my climb up the truck.

Cal was right there, hand out, and I reached for it.

It wasn't until he pulled me up to face him that I realized what I'd just done. But I pushed the notion away.

No reaching …

'You okay?' he asked, hands on my hips, keeping me steady.

I nodded quickly, adrenaline already rising.

'Follow me then.' He led me up and across the ladder, walking along it like I would a plank on a pirate ship, only there was a bucket with controls at the end. He opened the small gate and helped me in. 'You can hold on,' he said, pointing to the rail.

73

There was just enough space to fit the two of us. He gripped one of the levers and smiled at me. The moon shining down on his chiseled face made his white teeth sparkle. 'Ready to leave the world for a while?'

'Yes, please.'

He pushed the lever and the bucket jolted.

'It's alright,' Cal said in that soothing voice again. 'She's a bit jerky, but you're perfectly safe.'

I grabbed on to the railing and couldn't help but gasp when we swayed again, still going up. I tried to think of something other than the unnatural height we were climbing to.

'So, this is how you get cats out of trees, huh?'

'Yes, ma'am. Only the finest equipment for our feline friends.'

I looked down and saw the ladder I'd just walked across start to extend and go up . . . up . . . up . . .

'Oh, my God,' I breathed.

The few guys that stood by the truck got smaller and smaller as we rose higher and higher. We passed the roof of the firehouse and kept going. It wasn't until we were high enough to see the faint, dark purple of the horizon bleeding against the black night that I realized how far I could see.

Cal stopped the ascent. 'You're over a hundred feet off the ground.'

I could see the whole city and beyond. The moon was full and glowing, and I was surrounded by nothing but wide open night and Cal himself.

'Wow,' I said, taking in the incredible view, then the man who gave it to me. 'This is amazing.'

He looked right at me. 'Yes, amazing.'

'How do you do this?' I asked.

'You just push this button right here.'

'No, I mean this,' I stared out at the thin line of light beyond the darkness. 'How do you deliver on … everything?' Because that's what he did. In the time I'd known him, he always came through on what he promised. He also made a clear statement of what he couldn't do. But, in that moment, I didn't want to hide. Not from him. I felt too far away from earth and it eased my entire body, my chest finally able to take an honest deep breath.

'Tell me what you need and I'll do my best to give it to you,' he rasped and took a step closer. 'You just have to let me know.'

I stared at his mouth, and this time, it was me who took a step closer to him.

'It's nice not being a part of the world right now. I don't know if I want to go back,' I said.

He nodded and cupped my face. 'Reality is tough sometimes.'

It was all so simple up here. Just him and me standing in the night, seemingly floating through the sky. Just us. Just darkness. Twinkling lights of the city outstretched, filled with people and problems I didn't have to step foot in. I got to rise above. *Cal* rose me above. And for a moment, I truly felt like, if I closed my eyes, all wretched emotions would fade away.

'You can handle it, Lana,' he whispered. I opened my eyes to find him looking at my face, examining me with a gentle gaze. 'Whatever you're thinking about, whatever scares you and whatever you want to hide from, you can handle it.'

His faith in me rocked my ribs like a hit to the chest. I wanted to run, he let me, but he still thought me strong enough to tackle my world, one that I was hovering over.

'What if I don't want to go back down and handle it?'

'You always come down,' he said with a rough edge in his voice. 'Getting space and perspective is helpful, but the faster you run and the higher you climb just makes the crash harder to deal with.' He glanced out over the city and then back at me. 'And there's always a crash, Kitten.'

A streak of pain crossed his face, replaced quickly by anger, then some kind of solace. Whatever secrets he harbored, he dealt with them in his own way. There was so much that didn't make sense. Cal had a team of men around him that acted like a brotherhood. He had his aunt, who obviously loved him. He had support. What was he running from? Whatever it was, I believed him when he spoke of crashing. Falling was one thing, but hitting the ground was another.

I said his name, wanting to take some of the weight he carried, like he had taken some of mine. Leaning in, I whispered, 'Kiss me.'

He bent, and snagged my lips with his. So soft and quick I'd thought it imaginary. Just as my eyes closed, the bucket jolted, breaking the momentary feel of his mouth on mine.

Cal's hand was on the lever, and we started our descent down towards earth once more.

Chapter 7

After we came down, the crew put the truck back into the garage, and I locked myself in the bathroom and stared at my reflection. The buzzing ache of too many emotions wouldn't dissipate. Cal had taken me away for a few moments, and it was wonderful. But my feet were back on the ground and the lingering feel of his lips against mine wouldn't go away.

I left the bathroom and headed towards Cal's room right down the hall. It sounded like most of the guys were in the living room area, which was at the other end of the house.

Not Cal, he waited for me in the hall, just by his door.

'You ready for me to walk you home?'

'Not yet,' I said and bypassed him, walking myself into his room. He followed, and I shut the door. My system was overwhelmed with too many thoughts, wants, and needs. Primarily Cal.

I just wanted to feel something good. And Cal was beyond good. He was an escape I couldn't get anywhere else. He was the man I wanted in so many ways, but could only have in a few. So, I'd take the few I could get. At the very least, it would still be on my terms because my grand plan of staying friends was technically still in effect. Tonight, we'd just be special friends. That was logic enough for me.

'Lana? What are you—'

I raised to my tiptoes, slid my arms around him, and drew him down for a kiss. Praying to God he'd come through like he did that first night and hold me back. Only, this time, I wasn't letting go.

Clutching was different than reaching. And I was clutching the hell out of him.

'Lana,' he rasped against my mouth. 'You're upset and have had a hard night—'

'No excuses. Not tonight. You told me I couldn't give them, so you can't either. I know what I want.'

He stared at me hard, weighing my words, but I wasn't backing down. I was mad, sad, exhausted, and revved up all at the same time. The adrenaline I had building from the height I'd just been at, tied with the shitty aspect of today, was making me sizzle like an oiled cast-iron skillet.

I needed to unleash it all, and I wanted to be with Cal because he had been there from the beginning. He didn't let me hide, which was good, since I was looking for some control right then. Some way to take charge of the tiniest part of my world, if only for a moment.

'You told me all I had to do was ask? Tell you what I need?'

'And what is it you need?' he asked.

I pushed his chest until his legs hit the bed and he sat on the mattress. 'You.'

'Good,' he growled and wrapped his hand around my back, yanking me toward him. I instantly straddled his lap and kissed him hard and fast. Ripping off his shirt, my palms slapped on his chest, and I tried to push him to his back. He was too strong, and apparently wanted to stay sitting, because he wouldn't let me completely take charge.

He peeled off my shirt and unhooked my bra, burying his face in my breasts. I threaded my fingers in his hair and pulled him closer. He sucked the plump flesh all over, licking and biting every inch. He sucked on one spot, then moved down to suck on another, teasing me with how close he was to my nipple. But he just continued to taste, licking a perfect circle around the hard point, but never delivering the attention I was desperate for.

As his tongue slid along my skin, I arched my back at the perfect time, forcing that wicked tongue to drag across the pouting tip.

I gasped, the zap of heat shooting from my chest to my center.

A low hum broke his throat. 'Not in a patient mood tonight, I see?'

'No. No patience. Want you now.'

His answer was to clamp down on my nipple with his thumb and first finger so hard that it went numb. When he released it, blood rushed to the pouting point and he fastened his mouth over it, sucking and licking the sting away.

'Oh, God!' I moaned. I'd never felt anything like it. The sensation was so intense, alternating between pleasure and pain, and I couldn't think which part I liked better. All of it. Definitely, all of it.

He paused only to move to my other breast and do it all over again.

'Yes, yes, more.' I wanted hard, fast, and wild. I wanted to be gone from my world in every way possible. I may not be high in the air, but Cal made me high on something else. On the addiction to his touch. To the way he shut down my mind and bombarded me with feelings, not thoughts.

I was gone from reality and just existed as part of Cal. That's it. That passion that warred in my brain had officially been unleashed, and I wasn't holding back. I wasn't thinking of logic. All that would be dealt with later. Right now, I just wanted out of the terrible moment that came from earlier today at school.

The man's mouth was magic. And the way his kissed my skin made me feel sexy and wanted. Like he couldn't get enough.

He devoured my breasts with no sign of relenting, which was great with me. I leaned back, placing my hands behind me on his thighs to give him full access, which he took. Cupping them together, he sucked both nipples fast, back and forth, never leaving one unattended for too long. The zings of pleasure flooded my core, and I was already so wet that my panties slid across my sensitive flesh every time I rocked my hips.

'Off,' he said, reaching to unfasten my pants. 'Now.'

While he continued to deliver so much bliss on my sensitive breasts, I maneuvered my way out of my jeans and panties, which was no easy task, since Cal wouldn't let me too far from his mouth.

Now completely naked and resuming my position on his lap, I rocked against his hard cock, which was encased in his pants. Hating that there was still a barrier between us, I unbuckled his belt and got his pants low enough for his cock to spring free.

'I want you so much,' he said between licks at my breast. 'And for so fucking long I've wanted this ...' He latched onto my nipple and, as he did, he laid back, tugging me down with him.

I gasped at the delicious sting and even more erotic sight of him maneuvering me over him using only his mouth. I caught myself, bracing my hands on either side of his head before crashing atop him. He wasn't giving up my flesh. Callum appeared to be a breast man, and that was more than fine by me, because the way he tongued my skin had me on the brink of coming already.

As I leaned over him, he reached down and fingered my clit.

'Oh, God,' I moaned, the little jolt of pleasure was all I needed for a dose of lust to surge.

'Already wet for me, Kitten?' he said, and I could feel him grin against my skin. 'I want to feel it.' He parted my folds so that my clit was directly against his hard cock, then thrust slightly to run that hard shaft along my most sensitive spot.

'Cal,' I gasped his name. The feel of his ridged steel against my hot center made white flecks of pleasure pop behind my eyes.

I rocked against him, sliding myself up and down his length, my own moisture making a slick path and taking me higher and higher. With his hands on my hips, he continued to move me up and down, slowly, so that I could feel the entirety of him against my wet flesh without him actually breaching. His mouth found my nipple again and sucked.

I threw my head back, loving the bliss of being in control and on top while pleasure was delivered by a big strong man happy to give it.

He'd said he'd waited?

I thought of the first night we met. His kiss. How his body was so strong and I felt safe and weightless.

I was getting closer. Grinding my way to the brink of coming and not wanting to look back.

Just before I was there, Cal moved me. Holding onto my hips, he slid me up his body, my pussy running over very hard abdominal muscles, to his chest, then finally to his neck.

'You're not coming without me tasting it this time,' he rasped, and positioned my spread legs on either side of his head, my center in line with his mouth. With his hands splaying over my ass, he brought me down, sheathing me on his tongue.

'Oh, God, yes!'

He rocked me back and forth, helping me fuck his mouth. My hands flew to my breasts and cupped them, pinching my nipples a little and loving the wet sting Cal had left behind.

I whipped my hips faster, riding his tongue and getting lost to the amazing pleasure and power. He was so big, so strong, and yet I rode him. Sought my own pleasure while he laid there, giving it.

Out of the corner of my eye, I saw his biceps flex as he held me, his tattoo moving with every twitch of his muscles. Just the sight of all his sexy strength brought me higher. His hands left my skin, and I heard a rustling of clothes and rip of cellophane. I glanced behind me to find Cal had kicked off his pants and was putting on a condom.

Always loved a multi-tasker.

He licked wildly at my clit and the heat that had been building erupted to a boiling point. As he flicked the tiny bundle of nerves over and over, my orgasm swept me up like a tidal wave and crashed so hard that my entire body shuddered. Just as the intensity hit, his hands were back on my hips, and in one quick swoop, yanked me down his body, spearing me with his massive cock.

I screamed his name.

One second I was coming around his mouth, and now I was coming around his cock. And it didn't end.

He surged deep, his big hands encompassing my waist, bouncing me up and down as he thrust hard. It was too much and not enough, all at the same time. My inner walls were still spasming and milking him from what was an endless orgasm.

'Oh, Cal, it's not stopping.' I clawed at his chest, trying to find balance in any way I could.

'Good,' he said with a sly rasp.

I didn't know if the first orgasm stopped and new one began, or if it was all the same one, but a fresh dose of sparks lit up my skin and my body shot bright with pleasure. I couldn't hold myself up anymore. I leaned forward, my breasts meeting his chest, and he wrapped his arms around me, continuing to fuck me like he couldn't get enough. I couldn't get enough either, but I was reeling from an endless bombardment of ecstasy.

I let him take over. Let the pleasure roll over me with no way to prevent or stop any of it. And I didn't want to. It was unlike anything I'd ever felt.

I kissed him, soft and slow, so contradictory to how he was taking me. Fast and hard and completely.

'Say it, Lana,' he growled, pumping in and out.

My mouth didn't leave his, my lips resting on his like a pillow. I flicked my tongue, taking a taste of him.

'Say what?' I whispered.

He plunged his tongue into my mouth, taking all my breath and bringing on even more pleasure. I was lost. Consumed. Limp and happy to let him just take me. Fuck me. Kiss me. Own me however he wanted. I just took it. Couldn't think better or worse of it. I couldn't think at all.

'Tell me who makes you feel this way.' He thrust hard and stayed deep, stirring until I moaned.

'You do,' I said, kissing his lower lip. 'You do, Cal.'

With a groan, his body tensed, and he hugged me close as his cock twitched and jolted inside of me. I could feel his release through the condom, it was so powerful.

My entire body turned to liquid and I laid there, spread over him, and wrapped up in his strength.

My eyes were heavy, my body slaked, and my emotions fried. But I was in control.

I snuggled closer, his arms keeping me tight within his grasp. Reality hit me hard:

Cal let me come to him, let me be who I wanted and have at him the way I wanted. But in the end, he pushed my body to new heights while containing me within his grasp.

I may have been on top, but I was not in charge.

I quietly pulled on my shirt and zipped my jeans so slowly ... watching Cal the entire time, and hoping I didn't wake him.

He'd fallen asleep not long after the mind-blowing sex we'd shared, and I wasn't sure what to do now. Did I stay the night? Was that allowed? I at least wanted to make it to the bathroom and freshen up, then come back and talk to him.

Good plan.

It was getting later, and soon I was sure the crew would be coming down the hall to their own rooms to turn in. I needed to make it to the bathroom, then back to Cal as quickly as possible.

Tiptoeing out of the room, I closed the door behind me and let out a sigh when I saw a desolate hall. Just a few long strides and a hard right would take me to my destination. It also happened to be away from the area of the house everyone was hanging out in.

I hustled, while staying as quiet as I could. The end of the hall was in sight.

Hard right—

'Hey there,' Rhett said. 'Didn't know you were still here.'

Shit!

'Yeah, I ah . . . just was chatting with Cal about a few things.'

He nodded, but his expression told me he didn't buy my story for a second. I felt the urge to run a hand over my hair, but it wouldn't help. I was caught. We both knew it. Now it just depended on how gracefully I'd get out of this.

'Did you like the ladder?' he asked.

'Yes, it was fun.'

The way Rhett looked at me was odd. Not in a creepy way, but like he wanted to say something, then didn't. But he wasn't moving.

'I appreciate your help in making that happen. It's not every day I get to see the whole city from a hundred feet up.'

'Yeah, it's pretty cool.'

'Well, I was just heading—'

'Hey, Lana,' Rhett said, cutting me off. Something like pity streaked over his face. 'The guys will be coming this way. You may want to go out the back if you don't want anyone to see you.' He pointed in the opposite direction near the garage area. 'The gate is still open from earlier.'

I swallowed hard. I was about to tell him I was just going to the restroom and then heading back to Cal, when I realized that the situation I was in didn't look good. He thought I was trying to sneak out. Maybe I should be. Because maybe that was the routine?

I didn't know what to think, or say. If I thanked him for trying to keep my presence a secret that just confirmed that it was what I was doing. Sneaking out. Suddenly I felt . . . awful. I didn't know how to do this. How to have sex with someone, try not to feel, then walk away. It had taken me a long time to come to the realization that sex didn't have to be a dirty thing . . . so, why did I feel dirty?

Because I'm making myself feel this way.

What was my other option, though? Stay the night with Cal at the firehouse? No. I could have woken him up and asked him to walk me out, which he would have, with my head held high. But the guys would have likely thought exactly what Rhett was thinking right now. I was a woman traveling in and out of the shadows, hooking up with a fireman.

Rhett's offer was tempting to take. He seemed genuinely nice and looking to save me embarrassment. Judging by the way the guys messed with each other, there was a good chance I could be the butt of a joke, which was not what I was about to become. I couldn't help but wonder . . .

'Is this common?' I asked.

'Is what common?'

'Women sneaking out from the bedrooms?' It hurt to swallow, but I did and amended with, 'Cal's bedroom?'

That look of pity washed his face again. 'It's not uncommon,' he said in a soft tone.

I nodded, understanding completely. Obviously, Cal wasn't celibate. We weren't even committed on any kind of level. I'd also been warned that he wasn't a long-term kind of guy. But staring down one of his crewmates, stuck between exits, with my panties back in Cal's room, I'd never felt so stupid.

'Thank you for your discretion,' I said to Rhett. He nodded once, and I turned to head toward the garage the way he told me to go.

'Hey, Lana?'

I glanced at him over my shoulder just before I opened the door.

'Certain things with Cal may be common, but he's never thrown up the stick with a woman before.'

I frowned, then remembered that's what they'd called bringing the truck out and raising the ladder. I just gave a tight smile and nodded. I didn't know what to make of that. All I could think about was how I'd strayed from a plan that seemed to be a good one, which was staying strictly friends with Cal. Now, I was in uncharted territory and not sure how to react.

As I walked through the garage and out the gate, across the street, I realized that the uncharted territory had a name I'd heard before, just never thought I'd experience:

The walk of shame.

Sickness rose in my gut. Nothing about what I'd just shared with Cal or how he made me feel should be considered shameful. With him was the first time I'd felt warm and alive in a while. But my brain was a bitch, and all that passion I'd felt was now being drowned out by logic.

All my life I'd fought, tried, to be a 'normal woman' with 'normal experiences.' But if what Rhett said was true and this kind of thing was common, I didn't know if I could handle it. I was lost more than ever, and had no idea which direction to go in.

Chapter 8

'You all set to leave tomorrow?' I asked, keeping pace with Harper as we jogged down the street. Brown and gold leaves lined the sidewalks and crunched beneath our sneakers. Signs of fall turning into winter were everywhere, carried with the crisp breeze blowing the scent of snow off the Rockies.

'Yeah, it's not too late to change your mind and come with me,' she said.

I hadn't told her about Brock and that he was engaged to my thesis advisor. In fact, the only thing I'd really done in the past forty-eight hours was avoid Cal and try to get a frickin' grip on what the hell I was doing.

I was lost. And no matter how high I climbed or fast I ran, it didn't change that. So, I'd taken a different approach. Seclusion. At least until I could stop the spiral of emotions churning in my veins. It had been going great until Harper dragged me out for exercise and fresh air. Stupid nature.

'Thanks, but this project—'

'Yeah, yeah,' she said, as we rounded the corner. My project was my go-to answer for everything. It kept me busy. Kept my mind occupied. It was a blessing, and the one thing I was still attempting to have control over. But even that was tainted by Brock now. Instead of focusing on school, I thought about Erica, counting the days until Monday came and I could talk to her.

Our house was about five blocks away, and while getting out and letting the cold air hit my lungs felt good, I was eager to get back inside my bubble, effectively hiding from the hot firefighter I had as a neighbor.

Hiding.

The word burned my skull and I hated it. Despite trying to convince myself otherwise, which I had, with reasons like, 'Oh, I just need time to think because what started as awesome, ended with me feeling terrible,' or 'Oh, that intense orgasmic bliss left my brain cells scrambled, and I haven't been able to form sentences,' I was, in fact, hiding. I was also thinking about Cal way too much, and how having women sneak out of his room wasn't uncommon.

Was I just another one of his commonalities?

I didn't know. Which was why I was keeping my distance. Because friendship or not, I was wandering with no compass or clear path.

Deep breath. Cold air. Clarity. That's what I needed.

I had no right to feel jealous, or even wonder about anything Cal did, because we weren't together.

'I still can't believe you snuck out and ditched Cal the other night.'

I glared at Harper. Leave it to her to bring that up. Still, she had to be a mind reader. Either that or I wore my thoughts, because I had just been thinking the same thing. Even though it hadn't been my intention to sneak out and ditch him.

After the amazing sex, I'd realized that, once again, passion had overridden logic and, in turn, I lost my common sense. But I had been willing to stop and think. I just wanted to take a moment to reset and face Cal with a fresh face. Best laid plans turned into Cal staying asleep and me not returning. Thankfully, Rhett was a nice guy. But it was more than the involuntary sneaking that was a problem. It was the insanity.

I knew better. Knew what having an incredible night with a man you got lost in does to a soul. I knew how feeling less than enough, one of many, or confused in general tore at a heart. Problem was, deep down, I was doing all these things to myself. When I was with Jack, I was in a constant state of wonderment. Waiting for him to tell me how far we'd go and how close we'd get. But Cal was trying. It was *me* who was retreating. And it was *me* who spent the last two days avoiding his calls and texts.

'I have no idea what I'm doing,' I admitted, my breath fogging in the cold air as I spoke.

'You're living your life,' Harper said. 'There's nothing wrong with that.'

'But I know I'm handling this situation with Cal wrong, and yet I can't bring myself to face him or fix it.'

'What is there to fix?'

'Well, the fact that we had sex and we can't have any kind of relationship.'

'Why?'

I slowed and so did Harper. She looked at me like this was totally normal.

'Harp, I had sex with Cal ... and Jack.'

'Jack is gone.'

'I know!' Putting my hands on my hips, I caught my breath, and Harper faced me. 'It's not just that they're best friends, but there's other stuff going on too.'

'You mean that you like Cal and, on some level, trust him, and now you're terrified and running from him because you've been burned.' It wasn't a question, it was a statement. Because yes, that about summed it up.

'He has women visit often enough to where his buddies know the escape route to put them on.'

'What?' Harper asked.

'Nothing, I just don't want to be one of those women. One of many that creeps through the firehouse walls.' Especially when, despite my best efforts, I was feeling for Cal. 'I can't go through any more,' I said. I wasn't about to rehash the Brock issue, but the fact that I'd gone straight to Cal made me feel ... dependent. Something that left me feeling weak, and I didn't want that. I hated the thought. And yet, he made me feel wanted and safe at the same time. It was a line I hadn't figured out how to walk along yet.

'Cal and I give each other shit and yeah, we're not besties,' Harper started. 'But I know he actually thinks of you beyond a one night kind of thing. If he didn't, I would have said something.'

'You did say something,' I reminded her. 'Remember, when I first met him at the party in the park. You told me he's a runner. He's used to women that "know the drill."'

'All that is true.'

Frustration was rising. 'Then how do you know that he cares about me beyond a single night?'

Harper looked me dead in the eye, 'Because he put you first when it came to Jack.'

'What does that mean?' I said firmly.

'I guess there was an incident between Cal and Jack. I don't know exactly how it went down, but Cal stepped aside, so you could be with Jack. If he was trying to get into your pants, he would have already pursued you for just that and wouldn't have cared if you were with Jack or not.'

My mind raced, thinking back to when I was with Jack and Cal in the bar a couple months ago. When I'd realized they knew each other. Jack never told me the discussion they had outside, but whatever it was made Cal back off.

The other night, when I was wrapped up in Cal, he'd said that he'd waited for me ...

'How do you know this?'

'Rhett told me bits and pieces.'

'Rhett?' I asked. 'Are you two close? Was he the Viking?' Harper just stared at me. 'Harper? You really aren't going to tell me?'

'It's not that easy. Yes, Rhett and I are close,' she admitted. 'But I'm still figuring some stuff out.'

'Have I done something to make you feel like you can't talk to me about this?'

'No, of course not,' she said with sincerity. 'I just really need to figure this out on my own.'

I understood that. Despite how much I wanted to help, I had to trust Harper could take care of herself. Now, if only she thought the same about me.

'Rhett does seem like a good guy,' I offered.

She nodded.

But based on what she was saying, Rhett also knew a lot about Cal, and thanks to the other night, he knew a lot more about Cal and me specifically.

How had things gotten so messed up? Jack had wanted me once, enough to tell Cal to step back. Only, Jack left . . . he'd had a timeline from the beginning. It was yet another fork in the road that could have gone either way. But the way it went was with Jack. And I was left with pieces of who I was, pieces of who I was becoming, and Cal was the only kind of glue in sight.

I started running again, and Harper followed suit. I didn't know what to think or how to feel, other than even more lost than before. Wondering how things could have been different. But they weren't. And there was nothing Cal or I could do about it.

Problem was, I was feeling. Feeling more than I wanted to. Wanting more than I wanted to. Two things I'd tried to stay away from when it came to Cal, yet I was getting swept up, even though I knew better than to trust any part of myself to another person.

As we ran up toward our house, I noticed a black truck parked out front of the fire house and a few guys talking by the open doors.

Cal.

He was in street clothes and saw me, but didn't make a move. Harper, however, jogged right up to Rhett and started talking low in his ear, leaving me standing on the sidewalk, catching my breath.

'Rhett and I are going in for a snack,' Harper called, going with Rhett into the firehouse. Great. Just great. Best friend drops a bomb on me, then ditches me with the guy I've been avoiding.

A guy that seemed hell bent on stopping that cycle with every step he took toward me.

'Hey,' I said, as casually as I could. Cal didn't even blink. He didn't stop walking either until he was toe to toe with me.

'I told you once that running is one thing, hiding is another.' His blue eyes, for the first time ever, ignited with fury.

'I needed to think.' It was the most rehearsed answer I had. 'Besides, isn't that the status-quo? Great sex, then the woman sneaks out the back?'

'Finally, you say something that I agree with,' he said, and my heart dropped. 'The sex *was* great.'

Crossing my arms, I huffed, mostly to make sure my lungs were still working because he'd just scared me ... only to compliment our time together. This man drove me nuts.

'And there is no status-quo,' he continued. 'I thought you'd know that by now.' That blue glare only lit another degree. 'But, if that was a concern of yours, then communicate that, don't sneak off.'

I bit my lip, but kept eye contact. Looking away signaled weakness. Something I'd learned from Jack, but hated that it stuck in my mind. Now was not the time to digress. I was faced with Cal, had new information brought to light, time to ask. Otherwise, I would just stay lost in the worst way.

'What about *your* communication?' I asked. I lifted my chin, trying for any surge of strength I had. 'You stepped aside so Jack and I could be together?'

He took a deep breath through his nose, but didn't break eye contact. 'Timing is everything,' he said, and that rocked something in my chest. Jack had said damn near the same thing to me before turning his back and leaving for good.

'And who decides on this time? You and Jack? Things could have been different.'

'Yeah, they could have been. But did you ever think that you needed Jack more than you needed me?'

I gasped and rage surged through my blood like a drug. I wasn't some damn puzzle piece they could move around to see where I fit. 'You think you know what I need?'

'I've got a good idea. You *needed* to find your strength, feel safe. Jack is the perfect dark corner for that.'

There was that phrase again, dark corner. Even I'd admitted that Jack had been like that. And I did hide in him. I'd also found my strength in him. He broke my heart, but he also forced me to grow as a woman, as a person.

'So, you two just decided what you thought was best? Who would be better for me? And your conclusion was Jack? Despite him leaving in the end, you still thought that he was perfect for what I *needed*?' I snarled the last word. 'And what are you perfect for, huh Cal?' I stepped closer, anger and confusion all dueling at the realization of how out of control I felt.

'I think I showed you what I'm perfect for the other night.' The way his voice rolled over every syllable of that statement made my body flush with heat. 'You want a place to hide? That *was* Jack. And you're right, he's gone. But I'm the place you can run to. I'm also the one you run from.' He leaned in so his breath skated over my face. 'So, go ahead and run, Kitten. But don't think I won't chase you.'

Crazy lust and need swarmed over my entire body like bees to a hive. The passion was overruling the logic, and everything in me screamed for the chance to cling to power.

Find my control.

Force Cal's hand and call his bluff.

So, I turned and ran.

Chapter 9

My legs had never moved so fast. I sprinted toward the park that lined up with the fire station, then further, reaching the tree line that led into the forest. Faster and faster, I pumped my arms, the underbrush kicking up as I forced my body to move quicker and quicker.

Breathing hard, lungs aching from the cold air going in and out at this pace was like swallowing down ice crystals. But I kept going. Because no matter how cold the air was around me, my body was hot. A deep red hot I couldn't outrun.

But I had to try.

My skin was damp, but I kept going. I didn't chance to look behind me. I couldn't hear anything but the heartbeat in my ears.

Would Cal come for me?

A snap of a twig and heavy footfalls rang through the white noise of my mind, and I knew . . . he was coming.

And I wanted to be caught as much as I wanted to get away.

Because I knew that once he caught me, I just may let him have me. In a lot more ways than one.

I forced my legs to take longer strides, but before I could wind even deeper into the deserted forest, a strong arm wrapped around my middle, halting me instantly like I'd gotten strung up by an invisible wire.

'Quick little thing, aren't you?' Cal rasped, as he lifted me up and maneuvered me against the nearest tree. I struggled. Partly from the adrenaline and partly from the anger. Not at Cal, but at everything. At the situation. At the past. Just everything.

He grabbed my wrists and locked them over my head, his big body pinning me against the tree.

'Look at me,' he growled. 'You want to get away?'

I lifted my chin, but said nothing. The truth hit hard: No, I didn't want to get away.

'You want free, just say so,' he said again.

He breathed heavily against me, his strong chest rising and falling, skimming my breasts and making me hate the zip-up I had on and the barrier between us.

'I want to not want you the way I do,' I whispered.

With one hand still fastened around my wrists, the other cupped my throat. 'Say that again.'

'I want you,' I said. 'So much. But I wish I didn't.'

'Well, I'm set to change your mind about that.'

His lips took mine in a consuming, fierce way, and I gave myself up to it. To him. To his strength. Never once did he ask if I was scared. Never once did he question what I could or couldn't handle. He didn't worry about me like I was some fragile doll. In that, I found power.

Cal treated me like an equal. Like he needed me. Like I had some kind of power over him the way he had power over me.

I kissed him back. Wanting him. Just the way I'd admitted. Wanting him so much and hating that I already trusted him the way I did. Because he was right, I ran to him. And I ran from him. Yet, he came after me. Didn't turn his back. Didn't leave.

He chased.

I tried to get my hands free, and he finally let me. But he

looked surprise when I wasn't leaving, I was, instead, unfastening his belt.

'More,' I said, unhooking the clasp and shoving his jeans low on his hips. 'Now.' I grabbed his hard cock and he groaned.

'Love it when your claws come out,' he said, and bit my neck just before gripping my hips and spinning me around.

He peeled my pants down to my thighs, baring my ass, and pushed on my back. I bent over, grabbing the tree in front of me for support. The quick sound of a condom wrapper opening was all the preparation I had before he buried himself to the hilt.

'Ah, God!' I yelled. Driven by nothing more than instinct, I arched my back and pushed against him, wanting him deeper. Harder.

'Fuck, you're amazing,' he rasped, and slammed into me over and over. I cried out for more. Begged. It was rough, dirty, and I loved it. Neither of us were controlled, which was something I could work with. No preparation, just raw and wild and animalistic.

His hips slapping against my ass with every plunge into my body made me wetter just from the sound. Something Cal seemed to notice.

'Mmm, my little Kitten gets off on running from me, huh?' he said, fucking me even harder. He reached around with one hand and cupped my throat. 'Do you like being caught?'

'Yes,' I moaned.

'Tell me how much you like it.'

'So much, please more.'

'More?' He thrust deep and I called out his name. The hand on my throat reached to my lips and I sucked on his fingers. Now, newly wetted, he trailed his hand down, found my clit, and rubbed.

It was the flicker of fire I needed to heat my skin even further.

I begged for more. Couldn't get enough. I wanted to feel all his strength. His anger. His punishment. I wanted to feel the pain I caused him. Pain I'd been caused. All of it melded together into something I didn't understand, and I just wanted that sting of release. The line of pleasure and pain.

Cal's entire body was racked with tension, like he was holding back. So I pushed. Wanting him as far as he'd take me.

'Do you like me running from you?' I asked between gritted teeth. 'Do you want to punish me? Fuck me?'

A deep rasp broke from his throat.

'Do it,' I coaxed him.

He slammed into me harder.

'Do it,' I demanded again.

A whoosh of air sounded and his open palm came down on my ass.

'Yes!'

'Jesus,' he rasped, and I felt his cock get even harder as he continued thrusting. 'You like that?' he slapped my ass again. Then again. My entire core gripped down on his cock, tensing to come.

'I love it.' But I wasn't ready to give this up. I wanted to push for even more. 'But is that all you've got?' I looked over my shoulder and gave a little smile. He knew I was goading him, and the gleam in his eyes was so powerful it pricked my skin like needles.

'Oh, I've got more,' he said and wrapped my ponytail around his fist. He pistoned in and out of me so hard my teeth clattered while he rained spank after spank down on my ass.

Pleasure shot through every vein so densely that I thought my nerves would snap. I came hard and shivered with spicy chills from the intensity. Cal was right behind me, groaning to the sky as his pleasure overtook him.

With heavy breaths, he pulled me up until my back met his chest, while I was still cradling his cock between my legs.

He whispered in my ear, 'You can run anytime you want, Kitten.' He palmed my ass, the sting of where his hand was sparking another flicker of pleasure. 'Just know that I will always catch you.'

Chapter 10

'You've been doing all this by yourself for over two decades?' I asked, looking over Bea's shoulder as she showed me her bookkeeping for her business.

'Yes, a few years ago, Cal got me this computer and I keep all the accounting on that now.' She let out a noise that sounded like some wounded animal. 'It was awful to learn. But I have Facebook now too, so it was worth it.'

'Sounds like a fair trade.'

She swiveled her chair, gliding along the clear mat that laid over the brown shag carpet, and rolled to the bookcase.

'I like your home office,' I said, glancing around. It was dated and on the nineteen-seventies side, but still cozy, and all Bea. Two 8×10 photos hung on the wall. One was of Cal, the other of Jack. They had to be around ten years old. They looked so sweet. Cal smiled wide with sunny hair and bright blue eyes. Jack's black hair was combed to the side, like he tried to do it himself, and he gave a closed-lip grin. A balmy ache stirred in my stomach looking at them. I knew them. Saw the light and the hurt in their eyes. I may not have known the boys they were, but I knew the men they became, and my heart constricted.

'Thank you. I'm not much of decorator,' Bea said, scooting back to the desk while holding a large book. When she opened it,

I realized it was, in fact, a ledger. 'This is how I used to do all my accounting.'

'Wow.' She flipped a few pages so I could see how she organized every hour and dollar of her business. 'This is really incredible.'

'This is just writing stuff down,' she said. 'But if shadowing me helps with your project, I'm happy to have you.' She handed me the book and turned to the computer. 'I'm happy to have you without the project too.'

'I appreciate that.'

'I mean it, kiddo,' she swiveled again to face me, the little rolling wheels screeching as she did. 'You come here anytime you like, understand?'

Oxygen stuck to my throat and my ribs clamped down. I knew why Cal and Jack had the similarities they did. It came from Bea. She was their common denominator. Their protector.

'I understand,' I whispered.

'Good, now let's see here . . . oh, how about I show you 2012's records? It was one of our worst years, but we stayed afloat.'

'That would be wonderful.'

She pulled up a little footstool and I sat next to her as she started showing me through her documents. I was learning so much. Mostly that a single mother/aunt of two boys and a business she ran all her own was an amazing thing. This woman, singlehandedly, did it all and she did it with a smile and blunt honesty. It was so easy to turn away, take the easy route, and Bea seemed to always step up whenever the occasion called for it. Neither of my parents had ever done such a thing for anyone. Including their only daughter.

'Bea?' I said, just as she finished going over a spreadsheet.

'Yes, honey?'

'You are the one that impresses me,' I said.

A joyful, watery expression lit her face up and she threw those plump arms around my neck, smashing me against her.

It was one of the best hugs I'd ever had.

'Hey! Good to see you, Lana,' Dave said.

'Thanks, you too.'

'Looking for Cal? He's just right through here.' He ushered me into the firehouse and pointed at an open door off to the right. I hadn't been in that room yet, but apparently that's where Cal was. Most of the house was dark, the only light came from scattered rooms, which I assumed was where the guys were hanging out. I'd been nervous about coming here since last time. I hadn't seen Rhett, and judging by Dave's attitude, he didn't treat me any differently, so my hope was that I was in the clear, at least with my reputation and perception from the crew.

I pushed the door open a bit and leaned against the frame. A pair of large, defined, sexy as sin arms lifted two heavy dumbbells. I would know those arms anywhere. The tattoo along the bicep gave away that it was Cal. But all that tanned skin misted with a light sheen of sweat made me instantly salivate for a taste.

He was sitting, his back toward me, so I took a moment to appreciate the view before interrupting. Watching him do reps of bicep curls was redefining my definition of foreplay, because, holy God, I was getting hot just observing.

'Staring isn't very polite,' Cal said, and I could hear the smile in his voice.

'You caught me.' I walked in and around the chair to face him. He dropped the weights, stood, and gave me a hard kiss on the lips, like a couple would when greeting each other. But we weren't exactly a couple.

'How was hanging out with my aunt all day?' he asked.

'Good. She's amazing. How she kept track and on top of everything is mind blowing.'

'Yeah.' He patted my ass and sat back down, taking a drink from his water bottle before grabbing the weights once more. It was another casual gesture, like he just wanted to touch me and didn't need an excuse. I just continued to stand in front of him.

'I didn't mean to bother you during your workout.'

'You're not.' He started his reps again, and I realized that he had moved to the edge of his chair and with every curl of his bicep, brought his upper body a little closer to mine. 'You're inspiring me.' A wicked grin lined his lips and on the next curl, he nipped my hip bone.

I jumped from the little bite, heat instantly rising.

'I keep thinking about the other day in the woods,' he said. 'Can't jog through there anymore without getting turned on by every damn tree I see. Do you have any idea how difficult it is to run with a hard on?'

I laughed and he bit my hip again.

'It's not funny. I may never be able to go outside again.'

'Oh, you poor thing,' I said with exaggeration and straddled his lap. He instantly dropped the weights and those big hands landed heavy on my ass. 'I never meant to ruin you.'

'Well, that's what you're doing.' He pressed his lips against mine, his tongue tracing the seam, and I opened for him. Wasting no time, he tasted what I had to give him and moaned. 'Yeah . . . you're about to ruin this room for me too, Kitten.'

'Then I better get going.'

His grip tightened. 'I didn't say that was a bad thing. In fact, we should see how many rooms around here we can ruin.'

Cupping his face, I kissed his little grin and eased away. 'I just wanted to stop by and say hi and thank you for setting me up with your aunt.'

'Of course.' He tilted his head, those baby blues never leaving my face. 'Something else wrong?'

'I've just been thinking more about Monday. It's almost here. I'm going to tell Erica, and every time I try to think of the right thing to say, nothing seems . . . right.'

'That's because what happened to you isn't right, and this is a fucked up situation. But you're dealing with it and doing the *right* thing.'

An alarm blasted loudly throughout the entire firehouse.

Cal listened to the dispatcher come across the speakers with some code I didn't understand. He cursed under his breath and stood, gently sliding me off his lap and standing me to my feet.

'Car accident. I've got to run, Kitten.'

I nodded and he took off out the door and down the hall toward the trucks.

'Hey, you wanna see your boy in action? He's driving today,' Dave hollered as he ran past me, motioning me to follow. So I did. I'd never seen firemen jump to a call before.

I stood at the edge of the garage, out of the way, and watched how all of them worked like a well-oiled machine. Cal stripped down to his boxer briefs, just like the rest of the guys, and jumped into his boots and pants and had them up with his jacket and helmet on in five seconds flat.

Cal hustled to the driver side of the truck, then caught my eye. 'I'm here, Kitten. Whenever you need me. But you've got this,' he yelled over the sirens and climbed into the big truck. The ladder he once took me on proudly rested atop the truck.

With that, they took off, Dave and Mark waving from the back seat, while Cal drove the massive rig into the night.

He was so strong, so capable, and he believed in me.

I've got this . . .

*

105

It was finally Monday. A day I'd been anxiously dreading. With Harper gone for the holidays and Cal working the past several days, I'd spent the majority of my time alone, thinking of how to approach Erica.

There was no better way than to just come out and say it.

I walked into Erica's office and saw her sitting behind her desk.

'Hi,' I said. Her head snapped up and her eyes fastened on me. There was a softness in her expression, but her body language was odd.

'Lana, why don't you sit?' She motioned for me to do just that across the desk from her. Sitting may help me deliver the news I came to tell her.

I took a seat and clasped my hands in my lap. I'd been practicing what to say, how to broach this topic, but today none of my prep work made it easier.

'I wanted to talk to you about Brock,' I started, determined to keep things simple and stick with facts.

'Yes,' she said, as if expecting me to say that. 'I think that's a good idea.'

'Well, um, there's no easy way to say this, but Brock is not the person you think he is. When we were younger—'

'I'm going to stop you right there,' Erica said, her face a bit stern. 'Brock already told me about you two and your issues.'

Of course he did. Only I'm sure he gave Erica *his* version.

'It's more than issues,' I said.

'Listen, Lana, I think you're very smart, and your thesis proposal is strong, and I want you to do well. But I think it's best if you're assigned a new advisor.'

'What? Why?' I felt like the happy, breezy Erica I'd come to know was no longer the person I was talking to. The woman before me clearly didn't like me much at all. A lump rose in my throat as I realized that the rapport we once had was no longer present.

'Because we have a conflict of interest. Brock is my fiancé and your step-brother, and with your history . . . '

'What history did he tell you?'

A look of pity washed over her face and she leaned forward, her hands resting on her desk. 'He told me about the mental problems you've had. After your mother left and your dad married his mom, you had a hard time adjusting.' She reached out and patted my hand. 'It must have been difficult being a young adolescent.'

This was not happening. I knew, at some point, Brock would lie, but I hadn't expected him to go this far. To pre-discredit me. Though I shouldn't be surprised.

It took me several seconds to process what was happening, then finally, I figured the best way was to move forward with my plan of the truth. At the very least, she had to know. I couldn't walk away again and not say anything. Especially since she was closest to Brock and could get hurt.

'That's not what happened,' I said lowly. Anger hummed in my gut as I thought about how he'd sold this lie to Erica. How I'd have to be blunt and try to now sell her on my case instead of going in there with the only intention being the truth.

'Brock raped me,' I said plainly. 'What he did goes past "issues." He continues to torment me to this day, and what he's told you isn't the real truth.'

'Brock said you'd say that. Told me how much you went through when your mother left. I even understand, to an extent, how you craved the attention you'd lost. But this isn't the way to get it, Lana.'

'I'm not lying. Brock is not who you think he is.' My lungs burned. She didn't believe me. Refused to. I wasn't ready for that. I knew it would be difficult for her, but deep down, I thought she'd listen. I was wrong. 'The only reason he is dating you is to screw with my life. He's manipulative in every single thing he does.'

Erica paused, her expression one of hurt and sadness. 'I am trying to be sensitive to what you went through with your mom, Lana. But this needs to stop. Don't you see how this is tearing your family apart? How hard you're making things on Brock? He sees you struggle, and he is forced to pick up the pieces of his life when you go after him like this.'

'I go after him?' The words cut my throat as they came out, because I was certain nothing more hypocritical had ever been uttered.

'I know you struggle socially. I thought I could help, but at least I know the bigger picture now. I think it's just best we go our separate ways now.'

My mouth hung open, and I shook my head. Too dazed, startled and almost to a humorous melt down by how backwards this whole situation – conversation – was.

'You'll have a new advisor by next week. You'll continue to work with them on your thesis. I don't feel comfortable signing off on your project, since I won't be a part of it further, so I'll forward all your documents to your new advisor.'

'No, Erica, that's the least of my worries. I don't want you to get hurt the way he hurt me.'

'Enough.' She slapped her hand on the desk. 'My understanding only goes so far. The lies you tell about Brock end now. I won't sit here while you bash my fiancé.'

'Erica, please,' I whispered. 'I didn't mean to hurt you, but Brock is—'

'I won't say this again,' she said, her voice hard with concrete edges. 'No more talk of Brock, or I'll have to escalate this matter to the dean. For now, we'll part ways, you'll have a new advisor and can continue your work. If you take this further, I'll have no choice but to get the school involved.'

My entire chest felt as if it was going to short out. He'd completely charmed her before I had a chance to tell her the real truth. Now, everything was spinning. I worried about Erica, hated Brock for somehow working his way into my world once again, and school? The one place I had to myself? That I was thriving at? Was stalled. My project was halted, a new advisor was coming into the mix, and what about Erica? Would she be okay? I wanted to fight harder, make her listen, beg her to listen. Because, if Brock hurt her, I'd never forgive myself.

'I'm sorry for everything you've been through,' she said with sincerity. 'And I hope you find what it is you are searching for, but for the sake of my family, and our happiness, I truly think the best way to start to heal is by creating some distance professionally and personally.'

Despair closed in and the sting of tears barely threatened because it was eclipsed by crushing defeat and anger. Once again, I had gone up against Brock and lost. Erica was a genuinely nice person, and if anything happened to her ...

'Erica, I respect you and care, and I worry that—'

'There's no need to worry. Once the semester is over, maybe we can talk. Brock said he's open to family therapy,' she added with a hopeful gleam in her eyes. I bet he was. Another way to make me look like the crazy girl who cried rape.

'You'll get an email in the next couple days about the logistics of your new advisor and meeting time. Good luck to you, Lana,' she said, and once again I had been dismissed.

I stood slowly, knowing there was nothing I could say to convince her otherwise. The fiery sickness in my gut raged hotter and I wanted to scream and cry all at the same time. I felt powerless. The worst feeling in the world, and one I was familiar with.

Walking out of her office, I hustled out of the building and all but ran to my car. Getting in, I shut the door and took a deep breath.

A tap came at the window and I jumped.

Brock.

I rolled it down just an inch. 'Hey, sis, bad day?'

'You're disgusting.'

'Aw, that's not nice.' He glanced over his shoulder. 'Ball is in your court now. I'd be careful if I were you.'

'You threaten me even now?'

'Not threaten, just remind you of the facts.'

'Oh, I'm very aware of the facts. You may have everyone else blind to what you really are, but I know.'

'It doesn't matter what you know. Erica won't believe you. So, you even try to talk to her again about us, and that could be grounds for defamation of character. You really want to get kicked out of school?'

My breathing stalled. He held all the cards, and we both knew it. The truth was, school mattered so much to me, but my main concern was Erica.

'If you hurt her—'

'I love her,' Brock said. I scoffed because he didn't know the meaning. But, he liked threats? I'd have to sink to his level if it meant making sure Erica would be okay, even from a distance.

'You know that one wrong move on your part, one rough touch or evil glare, and her confidence in you will chip away. So, you so much as look at her wrong, make her feel unsafe, and she'll wonder if I'm the one to believe. You might be able to dress the part of the doting fiancée, but no one can keep up the façade forever. Not even you.'

His face turned a little red with rising anger. Oh, yeah, I could make threats too, asshole. Judging by the expression on his face, he knew what I said to be true.

'Which is why I won't hurt her,' he said with a sneer in his voice. I was upsetting him. He knew I was right, one wrong move and Erica would believe me. 'You know, maybe this has gone too far,' Brock said with a smile. I hated that smile. Because it always came with some trick or plot he had brewing. 'If you really can't get past what you *think* you remember, there are places for you to go to get mental help.'

'You intend to paint me crazy and lock me away in a hospital somewhere? You have no power over me.' Man, did it feel good to say that.

'I think that your father and, as of today, your previous advisor, would give compelling testimony that your issues have gone far past a healthy rationale.'

That was the final blow. Because the scary thing was, he was right. Everyone in my world would back him. Would assume I was the problem. Including my own father.

'I have people who believe me,' I countered, trying for any strength I had left.

He laughed. 'You mean your one friend Harper and Jack Powell? Harper would say anything to help you and doesn't hold much credit, and you set up a meeting with me and Powell. Most people wouldn't try to merge someone who supposedly raped them with their fuck buddy at the time, much less a business endeavor. Most people would be traumatized and stay away from the person who hurt them.'

'Oh, I've tried to stay away from you,' I said, my voice breaking. Brock was good at taking every ounce of strength I had. Yes, I had set up a meeting between my father, Brock, and Jack, but that was to get Brock to move back to New York and away from me. But that didn't change the fact that it still looked bad. And, once again, my father wouldn't support me if it came down to it.

I was powerless.

Without a family. Without a support system. I had Harper,

and she was the best friend I could ask for, but if ever I had a corner, dark or not, there was no one in it.

Would Cal be in it?

I shook my head and looked at Brock. No matter how small I felt, I couldn't let him see it. I couldn't let him think he was winning. I couldn't let him see me crumble.

'Just be smart, Lana. Use that brain of yours and keep your mouth shut, and everything will be fine.'

Story of my life. The one I'd been living since the night he took my sense of self. Something I was trying like hell to get back and hold on to.

I needed him to answer one question, though. I had just enough rage left to carry me through this conversation without causing me to burst into a panic attack or cry.

'You discredit me to everyone. You even try to sell me on the past with your distorted version by saying "you supposedly raped me."'

A small grin tugged his lips. He got off on this. Reminding me of what happened while discrediting it at the same time. But I pushed on, because I had to know.

'Have you lost your mind to the point that you believe your own lies?' I asked. 'Or do you just have a shitty memory?'

That grin turned to a full-on evil smile. His eyes scanned my body, the slow motion of his gaze on me made vomit rise, but he finally met my stare once more and said, 'There's nothing wrong with my memory.'

My chest split open, and it was all I could do to keep from shaking. He may not admit out loud, or to anyone else, what he'd done to me, but he knew. Admitted to it. And, somehow, that gave me the smallest ounce of strength.

It was real. It was horrible, but it had happened. And he knew it. That was worth the fight. The truth was worth the fight. All I had to do was figure out how to beat him before he took me down.

With a lecherous grin, he pushed back from my car. 'I'll see you around, sis,' he said, and started walking toward the building.

I started my car and sped toward home. My mind was in chaos, my entire world spinning off its axis.

Chapter 11

I pulled up to my house and saw a large firefighter sitting on my porch.

'What are you doing here?' I asked, getting out of my car with my things.

'I wanted to be here when you got home. I knew today was going to be hard.'

My pulse skipped. Cal had waited for me? Like he knew I'd need him. And I did. So much. I walked up to the house, unlocked it, and tossed my bag on the couch. I paced for God knows how long, the only thing getting accomplished was anger rising. I didn't know where to start. What to say.

'Lana?' he asked, trying to get my attention, while closing the front door and locking it. 'Are you—'

'I'm not okay,' I said, before he could ask.

'I can see that. What happened?'

I threw my hands up and paced some more. Adrenaline and rage were surging because I was not going to let weakness and fear take over. I needed to hold on to my frustration. Not the terror.

'Brock got to Erica before I did. He convinced her I'm the crazy one. I tried to tell her!' I hit the wall. 'I tried so hard to tell her, and she won't believe me.'

I hated the idea of her being with him alone. He could hurt her. And there was nothing I could say to her.

I knew I was throwing a fit, but everything in my body was going out of control. Brock was winning. Again. And this time an innocent person was caught in the middle. I dealt with him the best way I knew how. But bringing Erica into this wasn't okay. Messing with my life and threatening everything I worked for wasn't okay either.

'My family wasn't enough,' I said. 'My father wasn't enough. Tormenting me wasn't enough. He's going after my school, my dreams, and Erica is caught up in all this. If she gets hurt—'

'Shhh, hang on, Kitten,' Cal said in a soothing voice, catching me in the middle of one of my paces and pulling me into his arms. He cupped my face. 'You did everything you could. You told the truth, but you can't make people believe you. She's an adult and has to make the call for herself.'

'I hate this,' I whispered. 'It doesn't quit. This emptiness, this pain and fear and anger. It won't go away. Just when I think things are getting better . . .'

Something very serious and very sad crossed his features. He just continued holding my face and stroking my hair with his fingers.

'Why do I feel so out of control?'

'Because the world isn't fair and sometimes assholes get the upper hand.' He ran his thumb along my cheek. 'You're a fighter. He can't win over you. It may be hard now, but in the end: He. Won't. Win. Do you hear me?'

I shook my head, my teeth gritting together and my skin drumming with emotions. Once I was scared, hell, maybe a part of me still was, which was why I was mad. I was tired of being afraid. Tired of moving forward only to have the rug pulled out from under me. Tired of gaining a sense of calm and control and power, only to have it threatened.

I was so angry, the only thing I could hear was blood rushing to my ears.

'I want to fight. I want to scream and throw things,' I said.

'I know.'

I needed to get my power back. Nothing tonight had played out how I thought it would, and I was bone-chilling mad. And my heart felt on the brink of exploding.

I grabbed Cal's shirt in my fist and yanked him down for a kiss, only I bit his lips more than kissed them. He groaned, but pulled back.

'I don't think this is a good idea right now,' he said. Which only made my fury rise.

'Do you not want me?'

'It has nothing to do with that.'

I squared my shoulders and lifted my chin. 'You're not my corner to hide in, remember?'

His jaw clenched, clearly not liking me throwing his words back at him.

'I'm not looking to hide.' I gripped his shirt tighter and pushed so he walked backwards to my bedroom. When we near the bed, I unfastened his belt and tugged his shirt off. 'This is what I'm looking for,' I said, and kissed his bare chest. He was warm and hard, and I had way too many vicious feelings to be soft.

Running my hands along his chiseled torso, I licked and bit his pec, then sucked his nipple hard. His fingers dove into my hair and he groaned low.

'Whatever you want,' he groaned.

I couldn't get enough. With every swipe of my tongue, the fire of anger eased and the fire of lust rose. I needed Cal, and all his strength and understanding. Needed him to let me have him. To have me. Needed out of what had just happened and to escape.

I bit down his abs, taking each muscle into my mouth to suck briefly, and I traveled lower to his sexy hips.

'I want you so much,' I said, hitting my knees and licking the

116

V of his lower torso. I grabbed his jeans and yanked down, his cock springing free. I instantly sucked the massive head into my mouth.

'Fuck, Lana!' he cried to the ceiling. I loved hearing my name on his mouth, feeling all this strength within my grip. My control. It was drugging and I didn't know or care who I was turning into. I just knew that I needed Cal and wouldn't be sated until every ounce of aggression was worked out.

I sucked him deeper, tonguing along his impressive length as I went, looking up and watching his hard abs flex and that tattoo move as he tensed with pleasure. It was pleasure I was giving him. I needed an outlet, and he was it.

Taking his cock as deep as I could, I grabbed his ass in one hand, pulling him closer, while scouring my other down his stomach. He hissed. Little red welts were left where my fingernails made their path from his sternum to his hip.

He didn't try to thrust or take over. He just held on to my head, fingers wrapped in my hair and let me do what I wanted. Use him how I needed, and I did just that. And something deep in my chest warmed a degree. Cal was standing there, taking every single ounce of pain and frustration I had. Helping me. Taking the burden. Asking nothing in return.

No control. No dominance. Just let me feel how I felt.

I bobbed my head, taking him faster and deeper, pulling him as close as I could. I was ravenous, loving on his cock like it was the best thing in the world, because it was. I wanted to be everything he wanted. Wanted to control his pleasure.

I pulled away enough for him to pop from my mouth and I trailed my tongue down the outside of his shaft, not stopping until I hit the very base. I sucked and licked his balls, and that got his fingers in my hair to tighten.

'I'm so close,' he said.

'Good. I want you come for me.' I took his cock back into my mouth and sucked hard. He groaned and his release instantly hit the back of my throat.

His big body shuddered, all those muscles flexing, and I loved watching him come apart. Because of me. Because I pleasured him. Because I let him.

It was a heady idea, and a sense of power washed over me.

When he was spent, he cupped my face and raised me to stand.

'Lana,' he whispered, his eyes searching mine.

'There's nothing to say right now,' I whispered back and grabbed his wrists. His brows furrowed.

'Maybe not. But we're not done.'

He pulled off my shirt, then my pants, kicked his shoes and jeans all the way off and lifted me up and walked me to the bed. Throwing the covers back while balancing me in one arm, he laid me down.

'What are you doing?' I asked, as he climbed in with me and pulled the blankets up to our shoulders.

'I told you, we're not done.'

He pulled me close, those big arms wrapping around me. His warm chest pressed into my back and he hugged me tight. Though I was still in panties and a bra, he was naked, but made no move. He was still. Simply hugging me.

I squirmed a little because part of me wanted to get away. My mind was firing off random thoughts and emotions, and my body was slowly starting to tremble. Like I was chilled. But had no reason to be.

'Cal . . .' I squirmed, his grip didn't waver.

'You're going to crash from all the adrenaline,' he whispered into my ear. 'It's like coming down from a high, and it's going to hurt. The anger and rage and fuel you had will start to burn out and you'll feel . . .'

'Alone,' I said. Because the chills were getting worse. The magnitude of all the events tonight were weighing heavy. The blessed control and power I'd just felt was dwindling fast, leaving behind a sense of emptiness. My eyes hurt like they had been strained from holding back tears for days, maybe years.

'But you're not alone. I'm right here,' Cal whispered.

I nodded and gave myself over to the crash that was taking over my body. With my cheek against his forearm, I gently shook, and a single tear slipped out.

Cal just held me, and I prayed it was enough to fight the bone-chilling emptiness that was seeping into my veins.

Chapter 12

Chirp

My eyes struggled to open. A weird beeping sound broke through my sleep, coaxing me to wake up. But it wasn't my phone or my alarm.

Chirp.

I slowly opened my eyes. It almost sounded like a smoke detector. I sat up in bed and looked around. It was morning and I was alone. There was a large indent and ruffled sheets on the other side where Cal had been. For how long, I didn't know. Did he leave right after I dozed off? Maybe he was still here, just in a different room?

A flare of hope rose.

Grabbing my robe, I got up and walked through the house. Cal was gone. The chirp, however, looked to be coming from the alarm system. I reset it, assuming it probably got messed up when Cal left this morning.

I sat on the couch and replayed last night. A string of emotions flooded and none of it was logical. First, it sucked being ditched. It also didn't feel great to wonder if this was how Cal felt when I'd snuck out on him.

What was the hardest to process wasn't last night, but how Cal had handled it. He had known, sensed, what I was going through. He also knew what I had needed and let me have it. Then knew how to take care of me after. The way he talked about crashing from that kind of emotional high made me think he must know what it felt like. The man chased after fires for a living, so yeah, pretty sure he knew what an adrenaline crash was.

It was still nice to have him stick around for however long he had. I'd felt such a wide array of random feelings, I don't know what I would have done without him. It was becoming increasingly clear that how I handled things once, was not how I was handling them now. Timid, shy and afraid were not things I wanted to be. It made me cringe, thinking of how I was only a couple months ago when Brock had first moved back to town.

I refused to let him win or let him hurt anyone else.

A knock came at the door. I frowned and pulled the robe tighter as I looked through the peephole. It was Cal, holding up a bag of doughnuts in one hand and coffee in the other.

I smiled and opened the door.

'Morning, Kitten,' he said, kissing my cheek and handing me a warm cup of coffee. 'Thought breakfast would be necessary.'

'I thought you left.'

'Missed me bad, huh?'

I rolled my eyes and followed him into the kitchen. He was so comfortable in my home, and I couldn't help but like it. Like he wanted to be here. To be with me. Like he fit.

'Okay, so I've got everything from maple bars, to sprinkles, to old fashioned,' he said, motioning to the bag of heavenly smelling doughnuts.

'I'll take a sprinkled one please.'

He handed it to me, and I took it and my coffee and sat on the couch. He followed me. Bringing the entire bag with him.

'Thanks for this,' I said, taking a bite of breakfast.

'Anytime.'

It was funny how easy this was. Cal didn't seem like a big

121

cooker, but he was thoughtful. He went out and got us something to eat. Didn't completely ditch out. Not that I could have blamed him. Last night, I acted like a possessed person.

'Um, about last night . . .' I sat up and he faced me. 'I'm sorry if I was weird or over the top.'

'Don't ever be sorry for anything about what went down last night. Are you feeling better today?'

'Yeah. It's bizarre thinking back on it. I know I was angry and frustrated, but I felt alive and almost crazed with adrenaline. Even though all this negative stuff spurred these feelings, I needed to physically do something to feel better. I've had panic attacks before, but this was nothing like that. I just needed to take control somehow. Does that make any sense?'

'Yeah, it makes a lot of sense.'

How was this man with blue eyes, stubble, and casual charm still mysterious? I'd gotten a few hints over the months about him, but I wanted to know more. He knew exactly what to do last night, and exactly how to handle whatever it was I'd gone through.

'So, you've had these same kind of instances?' I asked, hoping for some more insight into the man I was growing closer to every day.

'I have. Adrenaline can be an addictive thing. It is also surprising. Sometimes just a spark is enough, other times it rages out of control. But chasing it can be half the fun. It can also sneak up on you.'

Yeah, last night was nothing I'd gone chasing after. I was hit with so many different things at once and just snapped.

'You're a chaser aren't you?' I asked, my mind flashing to last week in the woods when he'd done just that and caught me.

'I am,' he said with a low tone, as if thinking the same thing. 'Why?'

'Because the high can be amazing,' he said honestly, and his gaze seared straight to my soul. I hoped he was talking about me.

'So, like fires. You chase after fires,' I clarified.

'Fire is one thing, yes. It's dangerous. I have a sense of control based on training. While I'm in there, I know what to do, what's in my power, and I execute my job. But there's always a piece of it that is not up to me. I can contain the fire, not control it. No matter how hard I try.'

I swallowed down a big bite and looked at him with wide eyes. He could contain, not control. Made a lot of sense.

He reached forward and brushed a lock of hair behind my ear.

'The past happened. We can't hide from it or fix it. We can find things to help us cope. Help us move.'

'Not move on?' I asked, referring to what he had said to me on Halloween. It was the one thing that stuck out with me when it came to Cal. He never once had forced me in a single direction. Didn't tell me to move on from Brock, my past, my family, or even Jack. Simply to just move.

'Moving *on* isn't something I believe in.'

'You really don't think it's possible?'

'No. Anything overly painful or joyful leaves equal scars. So, you can move away from them, find ways to deal, but moving *on*? No.'

It was a bleak outlook, and yet freeing at the same time. I couldn't change the past, but I could grow as a person, which was the path I was fighting to stay on. A path that had gotten threatened and I'd lost myself.

But for now, I had Cal. He understood me on a level I didn't realized existed until this moment. Pain hurt. It was science. A reality. Love hurt. Maybe moving on was impossible, but using it to my advantage could be doable.

Brock won't win over you.

I agreed, because I wouldn't let him. We may be at a constant battle, but I wouldn't let him win.

'What are you moving away from when you chase?' I asked.

'Several things,' he said stiffly, as though my question seemed to hit something deep. Then he got up, brushing off his hands. 'I start a two on today. So, if you need me, I'll just be across the street.'

I gave a soft smile. He was clearly done talking about himself, and I was not even close to finished. I wanted to know more. How was he able to understand me? Why did he run? Why was he the way he was? The little information I had was a dangerous thing.

'By the way,' he said, kneeling in front of me to meet me eye to eye. 'How do you feel about turkey?'

Odd change of subject, but I answered, 'I feel fine about it.'

He smiled. 'Good, because my aunt is expecting you for Thanksgiving.'

He kissed my forehead, then headed toward the door.

'Wait, what? I can't just—'

'You really want to bail on my sweet Aunt Bea?' he said, guilt coating every word. I may not know the woman well, but she was tough as nails, despite her sweetness. His comment did effectively shut me up, though.

'I'll come pick you up. It'll just be the three of us. See you Thursday, Kitten.' Tossing me a wink over his shoulder, he shut the front door behind him, knowing full well that he'd just ordered a command, and damn if I wouldn't follow through.

I stared at the canned food aisle and attempted mental math. In one hand was cranberry sauce which was fourteen ounces and in my other hand, literally, was cranberries with juice that was twelve ounces.

I pursed my lips and looked at my options. Bea had said she needed two pounds of cranberries, but did she want that in sauce form? Or juice? And twelve ounces was a pound, right?

Ugh! I went back and forth. 'Maybe the sauce would be good . . .' I muttered to myself. Then looked at the other can. My lack of cooking skills were surpassed only by my lack of shopping skills. I had the basics down. Salads, yogurt, and the occasional hot pocket. Yeah, I ate like I still lived in the dorms, but, honestly, I'd never been taught how to shop or cook, so Harper and I just learned off each other. When I was young living with my dad, we had cup of noodles a lot, and after he married Anita, a cook was part of the staff. I showed up, ate, and left, no one caring or even at the table at the same time usually.

But, in this case, I was certain I could succeed. In my one foggy memory, my mother had cranberry sauce, and she cut it, there was no juice.

Sauce it was.

I grabbed two cans and put them in my little hand basket. I was actually getting excited about Thanksgiving. Bea and Cal were family, and inviting me into theirs for the day. I loved her house, her warmth, everything about the dynamic they had. She also trusted me with an ingredient for her cranberry sauce, so I was smiling like a goon.

I turned to walk toward the checkout when my stomach bottomed out. My chest felt like a metric ton of gravel had just been dumped on it.

'Dad?'

He faced me, his pressed suit and tie matching his seamless expression. 'Hello, Lana.'

I walked up to him faster than I'd meant to, and he took one step back. I glanced at his feet, hoping I hadn't seen that right. I was going to him, with some kind of . . . joy?

No, that couldn't be right. Last time I'd seen him, he'd lied to me, sold me out, and sent his wife to threaten me.

'I called you,' I said. It was after I had found out about Brock and Erica, and for some reason, thought my dad could help. Once again, I was wrong, since he didn't return my call or show any evidence of having interest in me whatsoever.

'I've heard of the issues with your brother, and I just wanted to make sure we were clear on a few things.'

'Brock is my step-brother,' I snapped. 'And you stalked me at the grocery store? Why not just call? Or come by? Or send your wife like last time.'

There was the anger I'd been missing. Funny how old habits die hard, and my first instinct was to run to my dad. He wouldn't be the one I'd run to, not now, or ever again.

'I came to find you,' he said, his voice lowering as he glanced around the canned food aisle. There were two people browsing at the other end, so we were relatively alone, why it mattered, I didn't know.

'You need to keep your mouth shut about Brock, about the past, about all of it.'

My forehead hurt with how hard I scowled. 'That's what you hunted me down to tell me?'

'Lana, just stay away. Stop talking. And stay away.'

'I have!' I snapped, those two people now turning our way. My father grabbed my elbow and ushered me further down the aisle and away from prying ears. 'The only reason I got involved was because Brock started coming to my school. He was messing with me before that, and you know it.'

My father just stared at me, a blank expression of unflappable stone.

'He's engaged to my advisor now. I had to tell her the truth. She didn't believe me anyway, so I don't know what your problem is.'

'Just don't say another word about it.' With that, he turned and walked off.

'Dad,' I called after him. He kept walking. My heart started to burn, but I called louder. 'Dad?'

He spun to face me. I held up my basket. 'Remember that one year we had Thanksgiving as a family? With Mom?'

He didn't say anything. I thought I saw him nod once, but surely I'd imagined it. So I continued with my line of questioning.

'Was it cranberry sauce or cranberry juice she bought?'

A flash of humanity crossed his face. For a split second, I saw my father. The man that once loved me. Once protected me.

'Sauce,' he said.

I nodded and watched him leave.

I should know by now that it never got easier seeing a man I once had faith in walk away.

Chapter 13

'Holy shit, you look incredible,' Cal said, standing on my stoop holding flowers. I looked down the front of myself. It was the first time I'd worn a dress in quite a while. It was tight through the bodice, but had a flowy skirt that hit just above my knees. The green fabric was a fall color, and I missed wearing dresses. Even though it was cold, the tall boots I wore would help, and I couldn't deny that I had gone through my entire closet twice searching for something to wear.

'You look pretty good yourself.' Cal's freshly shaved jaw looked sculpted and his eyes matched the blue button-up he wore with dark jeans. Damn, the man was fine. And I felt like a teenager getting picked up for a date.

'These are for you,' he said, and handed me the flowers. A small giggle accidentally slipped out. Yep, definitely acting like a teenager on a date. I couldn't help it, though.

'Thank you.' I put them in water quickly and grabbed my sweater and purse. When I turned back around, Cal was right there, in my space. His hand gently cupped the side of my neck, his thumb brushing over my earlobe.

'You're beautiful,' he said lowly. I looked up and all the air in my chest stilled. He looked so serious. And what was worse, he made me feel beautiful.

'Thank you,' I said again, only this time it was a whisper, and

I did so badly want to believe him. I wanted to lean in and get caught up and pretend for a moment that we were more than . . .

There was no label.

I didn't know what Cal and I were. Didn't know what to call our situation or even call him. With Jack, I'd needed clear lines and definitions. Somehow, with Cal, I'd just fallen into some kind of comfortable routine where I called, and he came. We were something . . . but I didn't know exactly what or how serious we were. And part of me didn't want to know. Because the deeper I fell, the more it would eventually hurt.

His lips brushed mine. Soft and so incredibly perfect that I forgot everything but the feel of his mouth. He could be so hard and strong. Take me in any way he wanted and yet, he chose to be soft.

Whatever road I was going down with him, it was a tricky one full of curves and potholes. And it scared me to death.

'You ready?' he asked. Though he meant for dinner, I couldn't help but apply it to my thoughts.

Was I ready?

I closed my eyes for a moment and took one step forward.

Moving . . . toward him.

'Yes, I'm ready.'

'Did you bring the cranberries, hun?' Bea asked, hugging both Cal and I as we walked through the door. The smell of roasting turkey wafted around us, and I inhaled deep the amazing richness of it.

'I did.' I held up the plastic grocery bag and Bea frowned. She pulled out the two cans I'd purchased and looked confused. 'Oh, no, did I get the wrong kind? Did you want them in juice? I should have gotten both.'

'No, no, this is fine,' Bea said, patting my shoulder. She led me to the kitchen where she had sugar, flour, and all kinds of spices on the counter. 'I was hoping you'd like to cook with me?'

Tingles hit my heart. 'Yes, I would love to.' Cal was already moving effortlessly without direction, grabbing the potatoes and going to work on skinning them.

'I can't cook worth a damn, but I can prep like nobody's business,' he said. 'And my mashed potatoes are amazing. Aren't they, Aunt Bea?'

'Yes, honey, amazing,' she said loudly. Then leaned in closer to me to say, 'That, and all that mashed potatoes require are a little muscle, milk, and butter. I give him the win, since he can handle those three things pretty well,' Bea whispered to me. It was funny how much the likeness between her and Cal came out when I least expected it.

Bea looked at the ingredients she'd laid out, then at the two cans I'd brought. 'You know, I bet the store is open for a few hours today. I'm just going to run real quick.'

'I can go,' I offered. 'What do you need?'

Her eyes softened and glanced between me and the cranberry cans. 'The sauce . . .' she said slowly, as if terrified to say the next words. 'The sauce I make calls for two pounds of fresh cranberries.'

'Fresh?' Oh, my God. I'd never felt like a bigger idiot in my life. 'I didn't know.' I wasn't sure if that last part came out loud, but that's what I was thinking. How did I not know that there was such a thing as fresh cranberries?

'I'm so sorry,' I started. 'I had a one track mind and thought that . . .' Thought that meager once upon a time dinner with my mother and father had been something special. It wasn't. It was out of a can. Processed and had a short shelf life once it was opened.

'I'm so sorry,' I whispered again, not sure what else to say.

Cal came to stand by me, potato in one hand, peeler in the

other, and was he wearing a yellow checkered apron. I didn't know when that had happened, but it was adorable. It also matched the one Bea wore. I realized right then that I may have been invited, but I was out of place. I didn't fit. Didn't know the routine or where to even start.

'Don't be sorry, Kitten,' he said and wrapped one of his big arms around me. 'I love this stuff.' He tapped the can of cranberry sauce with the peeler and looked at his aunt. 'Sorry, Aunt Bea, but I've got something to tell you . . .'

Her brow raised and I stood there, not knowing what to expect, but feeling like I should flee and spend Thanksgiving alone in a closet somewhere.

'I love this sauce,' Cal said, and tapped the can again. 'Yours is good, but this stuff is awesome.'

Bea tossed a hand towel on the counter, and a look of anger flashed over her face. 'Damn it, all this time I've been trying to convince you that my sauce is something special,' she said. 'But truth is, this stuff is better and way easier,' she hiked her thumb at the cans and winked at me. 'Callum, get the can opener. We're having Lana's cranberry sauce tonight.'

'Yes, ma'am,' he said, and fished the hand held opener out of the drawer and handed it to me.

'You two don't need to do this. I feel so silly that I didn't know. I can go to the store right now and we can make your homemade sauce.'

'Lana,' Bea said sternly, effectively making my mouth snap shut. 'We are having yours tonight. And it's going to be great.' That grave feeling I'd been carrying since I'd seen my father at the store a couple days ago started to scatter. They made me feel welcome, like I was part of their new tradition, and she gave up her world class cooking for my can. It was one of the kindest gestures I'd ever experienced.

131

'Thank you,' I whispered.

Bea just hugged me quickly, then cupped my arms. 'Look at it this way, we'll just make my stuff for Christmas.'

Christmas? That meant that she was expecting me. That Cal and I would last that long. I didn't know what to say, what to feel, other than blessed.

Truly blessed.

The next couple hours were filled with good food, and I was utterly stuffed.

'Dinner was amazing,' I said to Bea.

She wrapped her arm in mine and patted my hand as we walked toward the living room.

'Thank you, honey,' she said.

I peeked behind us at the kitchen. 'I don't mind cleaning up,' I offered for the third time.

'Oh, no, Cal cleans up. It's good for him.'

'I heard that,' Cal called from the kitchen, amid the sound of water running and scrubbing.

'Good. Now make sure you put all the leftovers in Tupperware to take home with you later too.'

'Yes, ma'am,' he called back. They had a dynamic that couldn't be matched. An honest caring for each other.

'Has this always been a tradition?' I asked, sitting next to Bea on the couch with the football game going for background noise.

'I cook, he cleans. Because, honey, I tried letting him cook, and it was a disaster. Only way I'll let him near the kitchen is with a sponge and soap.'

I laughed.

'How is your class going? Project work out alright?' she asked.

I glanced away, then forced a smile. 'Yes, my advisor loved the incorporation of your ideas. Thank you so much again.' Not a total lie. My advisor did like it, she just wasn't my advisor anymore.

'Of course. I'm happy to help.' She scooted a little closer then glanced over her shoulder to in the direction of the kitchen. 'Now, tell me,' she said in a hushed voice, 'How are things going with you and Cal?'

My brows shot into my hairline. I didn't know how to answer that. Seeing as how Cal and I weren't exactly dating, per se.

'Um, we're good. He's a great guy. Good friend.'

'Friend?' she said with disgust. 'If you two are just friends, then I need to teach you the art of reading men. Because Cal could wear a T-shirt that says 'She's Mine' across his chest and be less obvious.'

'Well, I mean we're . . . I don't know what we are.'

'Is it Jack?'

That made me almost gag. 'What do you mean?'

'I'm Cal's aunt, but Jackie spent most of his school days here, and I think of them both as my sons. I know him leaving must have been tough.'

My mouth hung open, and I had no idea what to say. Bea was blunt, that was no secret, and, if she knew I was with Jack, and now sort of dating or whatever Cal, what did she think of me?

'Honey, you looked spooked.' Her kind eyes studied me. 'I wasn't trying to sound like I was judging you. I just want you know that you're a part of my boys' world, which means you're a part of mine. I'm here if you need anything.'

That was the nicest, most unexpected thing anyone had ever said to me. And I had no idea what to do with it.

'Thank you,' I whispered. My brain churned fast. Maybe Bea was the person to ask about certain things, since she knew Cal on a level that no one else did. She also knew about Jack. Could I really take her up on her offer?

One way to find out.

'Actually, can I ask you something?'

'Of course,' she said with hopeful eyes.

'Am I ... doing something wrong?' It was the one question that had plagued my mind since day one, and it had gotten even louder over the past month. Jack and Cal. Cal and Jack. I didn't seem to fit anywhere, and felt like I was either missing a piece of the puzzle or just flat out ... wrong.

'Oh, no, honey, you're not doing anything wrong. Both boys are tough to understand in different ways. They also have different strengths, that's what balances them out. I may not have all the details on you and Jackie, but I know that you've been seen from the start. So, let yourself feel the way you feel.'

'Sometimes, I don't know what to feel. Or I feel too much.' That being a new development. 'And what do you mean I've been seen from the start?'

'I just know both of them noticed you right away. As far as the rest goes, trust your gut. There's nothing wrong with going for what you want.'

That was the problem. I didn't know what I wanted. I knew what I didn't want: being hurt again. Jack walking away had been one of the hardest things I'd lived through. Rebuilding with his best friend had some flaws in the concept. But with things so messy all the time, a place to land was something I cherished.

They balance each other out.

I thought about that statement. And about what Cal had said before about Jack. They both had strengths. Cal was the chaser, Jack was the corner.

'Is it hard with Jack being gone? I know he and Cal are close.' Funny thing, I was asking for Cal's sake, not for Jack's. When had that switched?

Bea just glanced around, as if Jack's presence was still in this room. 'We miss him,' she said simply. 'Cal and Jack are closer than brothers. They always come through in the end.'

134

That made me think that I was the issue. Something they had to get through. Was I hurting Cal? Was my presence keeping Jack and him on odd terms? I didn't know. But I couldn't take on Jack's burden. He left. It was up to him how to communicate with his family.

'I care about Cal very much,' I admitted. 'He makes everything seem . . . bearable.' I shook my head and rephrased. 'No, it's more than that. He makes everything wonderful.'

'Yes, he's good at that. I just wish he didn't seek the danger to get the calm.'

'Firefighting you mean?'

'Before that even. He was always looking for ways to give me a heart attack. Once he jumped off the roof with the hopes of making it to the tree. He missed and fell and broke his arm. That poor kid was hollering in pain and smiling at the same time.'

Sounded like Cal. It also sounded like what he'd told me a few days ago about overwhelming emotions and chasing after a high.

Apparently, he'd been chasing a high since he was a kid.

'Why would he do those things?'

'His mother's passing was hard on him,' she said quickly, like it was a recited answer she'd given several times in the past. I recognized it because I'd done the same. Rehearsed speeches I'd give myself to deal with what Brock had done to me.

'May I ask how she died?' Bea's eyes lined with tears. I felt instantly horrible. 'Oh, my gosh, I'm so sorry. Forgive me for being so rude. I just—'

'You just want to know Cal better, I know,' she said with a watery smile. 'My sister battled addiction. A battle she lost in the end.'

'I'm so sorry,' I said. Though the details still weren't clear, I wasn't about to ask any more. I hugged Bea, and she hugged me back.

'You're a good girl, honey,' she said, and rubbed my back. 'I hope you know that.'

Her words pricked something in my heart that had long ago stopped working. She thought I was good? Thought me worthwhile for not just Jack, but Cal?

'Whoa, I leave you two alone for ten minutes and you're crying?' Cal said, walking into the living room.

'Oh, hush, I'm not crying,' Bea said, pulling away and running her fingers under her eyes.

'I was hoping to get some dirt on you,' I said to Cal, trying to lighten the mood.

'Oh! I have scrapbooks!' Bea piped up with a smile, seeming to like this direction of conversation much better than the other.

'No,' Cal said calmly.

'And some VHS tapes of his school play!'

'No.'

'Ooh! And I even think I saved that thing you had growing on the back of your scalp,' Bea said with excitement, as she scuttled down the hall and flung open the closet door.

'Thing growing?' I asked Cal.

He sighed and pinched his nose.

'Here it is!' she waved the—

'Oh, my God, is that a rat tail? You had a braided rat tail?' I said with disbelief and amusement.

'It was awesome at the time,' he defended.

'And what time was that? 1988?'

'I was a bit behind in the trends.'

Bea came out with a box of stuff and two scrapbooks.

'Aunt Bea, I thought we talked about you needing to get your hoarding under control,' Cal said, now blushing.

'I only hoard the wonderful stuff. Like this!' She held up a glittery mask with macaroni glued to it. 'It was your superhero mask when you were seven.'

I settled in as Bea opened the scrapbook. Cal groaned and sat in the chair next to us. I smiled at him as Bea started telling me the background of each and every picture.

'This really isn't fair. Just wait until I get the dirt on you,' Cal said with a wink to me. I smiled back, but something in my heart hurt. My father was barely speaking to me, and only to tell me to stay away. My mother hadn't called me in over a year. It was safe to say there were no scrapbooks or painted masks in my past.

So, I sat there, letting myself get caught up in the happiness of Bea and looking through pictures of Cal and wondered if this was what it felt like to be a part of a family.

Chapter 14

'You want to stay at my place tonight?' Cal asked, gripping the steering wheel of his truck and looking out the window as we drove away from Aunt Bea's.

'At the fire station?'

'No, I have an actual home. And I'm off tomorrow.'

Wow, I hadn't seen Cal's *actual* house. He'd mentioned it before, but it was this phantom thing in the background.

'Stay at your place, like stay the night?'

'Yep. None of that ducking out like you did at the station that one time either.'

'Hey, I stayed the last time we, ah . . .'

'Had sex.'

'Yeah.'

'That's because we were in *your* house, Kitten. This time, you'll be in mine, and I already have doughnuts on hand, so I won't have to leave.'

He was so easy to fall into pace with. Like hanging out, having sex, going to Thanksgiving dinner with his aunt, and staying the night at his house were all normal, simple things that didn't need to be overthought. Which I liked. A lot. Because my brain was weighed down with so much stress. But Cal just made things easy – didn't make me feel like I was clinging to mixed messages or afraid of losing.

Which was not smart. I've lost, big. Losing Cal would be difficult. He was a wonderful friend ... boyfriend? I had no idea. But he made me feel safe and he listened to me. He understood me on a level I didn't because a lot of the issues I was going through were new.

'You've got me on pins and needles over here, Kitten. It's not like I asked you to move in. It's one night.'

'Yeah, that's what I was thinking about.'

'Is this a big decision that merits a lot of thinking?' He wasn't asking rudely, he sounded genuinely curious.

'I don't know. I was just wondering how all this looks. And what I'm supposed to say when I get asked certain questions.'

'Shit,' he whispered. 'Bea was grilling ya, huh?'

'It's not that. She was great. But she did ask about us, and I said you were a great friend.'

'Ouch.'

'What? That's what we are, right?'

'Oh, totally,' he said with sarcasm. 'Yeah, when you're clawing at my hair and coming hard around my cock that's the first thing I think of: What a great friend you are.'

'I didn't mean it like that.'

'Is there something more you want?'

I opened my mouth, then shut it, because I didn't know. What we had felt like it was more. But there was no title, which was part of the reason I'd been able to deal with it. Because if I really moved toward Cal and away from Jack and solidified things, it would change everything.

Wasn't everything already changing, though?

I ran a finger along my temple, warding off the oncoming headache. Changing or not, some facts were inescapable.

'Jack is coming back here someday,' I said quietly.

'I see. You want to be available for him.'

'No. That's not it. I'm just trying to be realistic. You two are close. Your Aunt is close with him. If we are together or whatever, and he's back, how is that going to be? How will that work?'

Cal's jaw was set, his eyes staring out the front window.

'We'll deal with that when it happens,' he said.

'That's a big issue to tackle.'

'There's only something to tackle if you want more with me.' He glanced my way. 'Do you?'

The ridges and smooth line of his handsome face were impossible not to get caught up in. But he sat, waiting. He was so still when everything was scrambled and messy, but the only truth I could find was, 'It feels like we already have more.'

That got him to really look at me for a moment. 'Yeah, it does.'

I wanted to be with Cal. But there was so much that was out of my control, an issue I was already struggling with. The idea of being without him? The idea of not being able to see him, hear his voice, or run into his arms made me feel cold.

Cold.

The one measurement Jack taught me to take my feelings against. Cal made me feel warm, that was something to work with. The second things went cold, that was unworkable.

I closed my eyes for a moment, wondering if Jack would ever totally be out of my head. Certain things he'd said and taught me, forced me to realize my own strength and limits. And Cal let me claw for my own sense of control and strength.

Despite all the drama that surrounded us – the disaster that surrounded me – one thing I was sure about: I wanted to know Cal more. I wanted to be a part of his world.

'I'd like to stay at your place tonight,' I said.

Cal smiled and took the next right.

'Your home is beautiful,' I said, walking around the open floor plan. It was a single level, but large, and sat on a couple of acres.

Nice thing about Colorado was that while he was still close to town, he had his own space.

The back windows were large and the sliding glass door led to an open field with not another house in sight. The entire place was cozy meets bachelor pad, and the smell of leather and pine wafted around like the house came with its own signature scent.

A big cream sectional couch was faced toward the TV, and the cushions were so large and fluffy it looked more like an awesome L-shaped bed than a couch.

'I'm glad you like it,' he said, bringing me a mug of tea. 'You look tired.'

'Yeah, I know.'

I hadn't slept a whole night through in a while. There were sleeping pills in my purse I'd had for a couple weeks, but I hadn't taken them yet. I've never taken any kind of prescription for sleeping, so I was nervous. Plus, I was holding on to wishful thinking that I could somehow beat the stress in my mind and actually fall into a deep sleep. So far, no luck.

'You want to go to bed?'

'Actually, I want to talk to you.'

'Okay.' He sat down and I did too, curling my legs on the couch and holding my warm mug between my hands.

'What are we doing?' If there was one thing I'd take away from Bea it would be bluntness.

He looked at me, confused. 'Ah, I thought we were talking?'

'Yeah, but I've tried holding out, rolling with this situation, but the way you say things sometimes makes me realize that we're not normal.'

He grinned. 'I've never been accused of being normal, Kitten.'

'You just say things like, "want to go to bed" as if we're a couple and we're going to just ...'

'Go to bed?' he finished.

'Yeah.'

'And that's not normal?'

'No. I mean, yes, it is, for some people. But you're not like "oh, baby, let's fuck, then you can leave."' I made my voice exaggeratingly deep on the last part.

'Because I don't want you to leave,' he said.

'Right! See how this is tricky?'

'Not really.'

He just took a sip of his drink, as if calmly waiting for me to sort out my crazy. 'It's pretty simple, Lana. You tell me what you want. And that's what we do. I thought I'd said this before . . . ' he tapped his cup, then nodded. 'Yep, I have.'

Oh, so he was getting sassy now. He just grinned and continued to be casual, without a care in the world. It hit me that I'd been thinking of this backwards.

With Jack, things were so different. I needed answers and his confirmation on everything. He was in control and I felt like I was trying to keep up, trying for more, and didn't know where the lines were. But he kept me in check, and I trusted him blindly.

With Cal, he was every bit as alpha as they came, but let me feel and be however I wanted. He didn't keep me in check, he caught me when I crashed. Letting me feel and fall, but supporting me when I did.

'I want to know what you want,' I said.

Cal and I had been dancing around each other for a while. From how we first met to now, nothing was typical. But I needed to know the end result. Because there would be one. That was one thing I'd learned the hard way a couple months ago.

'I want you, Lana.' His voice was raspy, and the way he said that and my name made me really believe him. 'The future will be complicated because Jack will be a factor. A prevalent one,' he said. But how he said it made me pause. Like he knew something

I didn't. Like maybe when Jack was supposed to come home? I wanted to ask questions, but didn't want to hurt Cal's feelings.

'What?' he asked. 'You look like you're going to chew your lips off. Say what you need to say.'

There it was. Once again, something Jack had once said to me. There were moments I realized how similar things were, how they both were observant and seemed to read me, just in different ways. In those moments, it made my heart stall because I thought of Cal and Jack, and didn't know how to respond.

'Does Jack know about us?'

Cal took a deep breath. 'Yes.'

My lips parted. I wanted to berate Cal with more questions. Like, did he care? When he got home, what would happen? Would I have to see him? Do Cal and I even have long term capabilities?

'You want to know everything?' Cal asked with a slight angry rasp. 'Want to know what he said?'

He was the one here. He was the one that fought for me, held me, and lifted me up. While a piece of my heart was with Jack, I couldn't bear to know what he said. For both Cal and my sake, I shook my head.

'No. I don't want to know.'

Cal sat back. It was now or never. Time to see just what *more* we were talking about and if we'd survive it. Just one time, I had to say the truth out loud if there was a real chance moving could be possible.

'I trusted Jack,' I admitted. 'I loved him.'

'I know.'

'He's your best friend.'

'I know that too.'

'So . . . how can you and I ever really—'

'It will be difficult. You're right, Jack will come back. His home

143

is here. And when he does, we'll have some issues to face. Being naïve to that is a waste of time. But what I want is you. Now. The rest we'll deal with when it happens.'

After Jack, I learned that the best laid plans with promises didn't even work. So Cal's notion of flying by the seat of our pants and dealing with it as it came was just as sound of a method to attempt as any other.

I set my tea down on the coffee table and rose. 'I'm ready for bed.'

Heat smoldered behind his eyes and he pushed to his feet and picked me up like a princess. I laughed and wrapped my arms around his neck.

'I can walk, you know?'

'Perks of dating a firefighter,' he said, carrying me toward the bedroom.

'So, we're dating . . .' I said with a raised brow.

'We're about to be doing a lot more than that, Kitten.' He kissed me quick, then pushed open his bedroom door with his foot and entered.

It was large with soft cream carpet and wood furnishings. But everything looked rustic and made from actual tree stumps and limbs. Like a cozy cottage. The massive bed had dark blue sheets and pillows, and everything about his room screamed mountain getaway. I loved it.

'You know, I've got nothing to sleep in.'

'Exactly,' he said with a smile.

I shimmied down and he let me. One of the best things about Cal was that he was playful and easy. But I had yet to really reciprocate that playfulness. Something I was going to rectify, because I wanted this good mood to last.

'Well, you leave me no choice, I'm going to have to steal something from you,' I said.

'It's only fair,' he agreed.

I faced him and gently ran my hands beneath his shirt and up his torso. 'You should not be wearing all these clothes if we're set to go to bed.'

'Yes, ma'am.'

I stepped back and watched him kick off his boots, unbutton the first several buttons of his shirt, then peel it over his head, leaving him in bare feet and jeans with a wickedly hot black leather belt.

'Hang on,' I said, taking my time to look him over. His tattoo alone was drool-worthy and I just stood there, ogling him.

'Getting a good look, Kitten?'

'Yes, I am,' I said with no shame. 'Now, do a little spin.'

'Yes, ma'am.' And he did just that, slow and exaggerated, and finally faced me again. 'Mmm, mighty fine package you are, Mr. Malone.'

'Are you trying to make me blush?'

'Maybe a little,' I said. Then I lifted my chin, motioning at his pants. 'Off with those. Then you can get in bed while I try to find something suitable.'

'Ordering me around is fine for now, Kitten,' he said, unbuckling his belt. 'But the second you bring that sweet ass of yours into *my* bed, all bets are off.'

His words sparked lust and need so hot and wet I was ready to jump on him right then. But this was too fun. I'd never had a boyfriend I could have fun with. To tease and feel like a vixen, which was what I was going for. It was freeing and nice.

He sat on his bed, stretching out in nothing but his black boxer briefs and threaded his fingers, bringing them behind his head. He laid there, simply watching me. I couldn't help but want to take my playing to a naughtier level.

I walked toward the large dresser that was made of the same

wood as his bed and opened the first drawer. My back was toward him, and I may have swung my hips a little extra as I perused the contents.

'Uh oh, found your unmentionables,' I said with a grin over my shoulder. I gave an exaggerated sigh. 'I need to get out of this dress.' Then peeled it down my shoulders and off, keeping my back toward him the whole time. When it pooled at my feet, I stepped from it and bent over to unclasp my heels.

Cal hissed. 'Fuck me, woman, your teasing is torture.'

I stepped out of my heels, leaving me in my bra and lace thong, and I looked at him. He was still laying back, his eyes trailing over every ounce of skin, and his boxer briefs were now tented. Just bending over got him hard? That made me feel pretty good, since just the sight of him gave me goose bumps.

I spun back toward his dresser and opened the next drawer. T-shirts. I pulled one of the Golden Fire ones out and held it up.

'Do you mind if I borrow this?'

'Not at all.'

Facing him. I unclasped my bra and let it fall to the floor. 'That feels better,' I said, cupping my breasts once, to which Cal sat forward and groaned. Just his eyes on me had me wet and my nipples hard. I'd never felt so free, yet in control. It was amazing what finding some confidence in my body did. Because Cal made me feel like just the sight of me was worth waiting for.

Hooking my thumbs in my panties, I slid them down and off.

Grabbing the T-shirt, I put it on.

'Gotta say, Kitten. I'm not a fan of covering you up, but seeing you in my shirt?' He ran a palm down his very noticeably hard cock. 'That's a new level of sexy.'

I took a single step toward the bed. 'Those need to come off,' I said, motioning to his underwear.

He did just as I asked.

Holy mother of God, the man was made from fantasy. He was strong and powerful, and my mouth watered remembering the taste of him. The feel of him.

I took another step, drunk on the slow, seductive power he was giving me.

'Will you touch yourself?' I asked.

I wanted to see how he liked to be touched.

He gripped his cock in his fist, but didn't move it.

'Will you?' he countered.

I licked my bottom lip and trailed my hand down my stomach. His shirt was so big on me that it hit my thighs, so I gathered the material in my fist, pulling up the hem so he could see between my legs.

With my other hand, I covered my core. He hissed a breath and stroked once. I dipped between my folds, surprised at how wet I already was, and circled my clit slowly.

He ran his fist up and down his cock, his bicep bulging with each glide.

I took another step, continuing my slow self-pleasure.

'Every night,' he rasped. 'Since the moment I met you, I've made myself come to thoughts of you.' He stroked again. 'Never imagined it'd be like this.' His voice was hoarse and his eyes were searing.

Another step.

'What did you think of?' I asked.

His stare stayed locked on me while his hand worked himself in time with mine. Looking at each other while touching ourselves was intimate on a level I hadn't realized.

'I thought of your face. How you'd look at me when I was inside of you. How your lips would part and you'd gasp. How you'd call out my name when your tight pussy got so hot and wet for me. How you'd taste . . . '

My fingers worked faster.

'You thought of all that?'

He nodded.

He thought of me before we were together. Before Jack. Before everything. And I believed him. Because the way he was looking at me now, the way he'd been honest with me, made everything melt away and all I could see, all I could want, was him.

'I want to feel you,' I said. 'All of you . . . if that's possible?'

'All of me? As in, no barrier?'

I nodded. I had only been with Jack and I'd gotten checked after he left. Not that I thought he'd ever lie to me about being healthy, but just for precaution. 'I'm on birth control and healthy.'

'I'm clean too.'

I nodded, realizing how much I did trust him. And I wanted to feel him, connect with him on a level that went beyond.

I watched his hand work his cock. He was so hard, and I wanted to feel his flesh against mine. Just the sight of him had me circling toward a building orgasm, but I wanted to be with him and let him take me the rest of the way. So I slid my knee onto the mattress and, in an instant, he cupped my hip and dragged me beneath him.

'I told you, Kitten,' he kicked my legs apart with his knees, 'the second you got on this bed, you're mine.' His arms laced under mine, he grabbed the sheets and pulled himself inside of me.

I gasped his name and held tightly to his back. He didn't waste time. Just saw me, took, and we were now connected.

'Fuck, you feel amazing,' he groaned.

Wrapped up in all his strength, feeling him so completely was like getting lost in the best way. I didn't have to think. Didn't have to worry or wonder about the future or the what if's of my life. I just had to lay there, and take everything Cal gave me.

He kissed me hard, surging even harder. All the pent up

148

questions and insecurities melted away. I just wanted him. I pushed against him to sit up. He didn't miss a beat. Never leaving my body, he grabbed me and moved to sit up. With his back against the headboard of the bed and me straddling him, he buried his face in my neck and thrust up.

'Oh, yes,' I said. So he did it again, my breasts bouncing with each plunge. I grabbed the headboard and slammed my hips down just as his came up, hitting so deep I cried out from the pleasure.

'That's it,' he rasped, and yanked up my shirt to bare one of my breasts. 'Fuck me how you want.' He latched onto my nipple and sucked. The sensation mixed with the hard power of his body working in and out of mine was so dizzying I couldn't see straight.

Gripping the headboard, I bore down on him, whipping my hips in his lap as he pumped in and out, hitting every single spot I had and flying me over the release.

'Cal, yes, oh God, Cal.'

He growled and now I knew why. He'd imagined what his name sounded like when I called it out. So I did it again. And again.

'I'm going to come, love,' he said, and buried his face in my neck. I hugged him tight and his whole body shuddered. His hot release flooded me and hit so deep my inner walls spasmed again, as if wanting more.

Cupping my face, he peppered kisses along my mouth, my jaw, and my neck. Loving on me like I had done something special. It was sex. We both knew that. But this time, it went further. From playful, to serious, to intimate. It was new. Different. Yet completely ours.

'I'm glad you invited me over,' I said with a smile and heavy breathing.

'Oh, Kitten, you have no idea how glad I am you accepted.'

Chapter 15

I tossed and turned for the millionth time. It was almost two a.m., and after the amazing sex, I was sure I'd be able to sleep. No such luck. My mind just wandered with more thoughts than I could process. I was so tired I couldn't think, yet my brain wouldn't shut off.

I quietly slipped from Cal's bed and turned to look at him. His arm was out, as if seeking the empty sheets of where I'd just been. He looked so peaceful. So incredibly handsome.

I walked to the front room where I'd left my purse and got the sleeping pills out that the doctor prescribed me a few weeks ago.

I just wanted some rest. I wanted to be able to wake up with Cal tomorrow and not feel exhausted, and maybe even enjoy the day.

'Take one to two ...' I read. I popped two in my mouth, grabbed a quick drink, and put the pills back in my purse. I headed back to bed and snuggled in next to Cal. Even in his sleep, he reached for me and pulled me close. His body was like a furnace, running hot and warming me, so I didn't bother with covers. I just closed my eyes, tried to let my mind go blank, and prayed for sleep to finally come.

'Lana ...'

I heard Cal calling my name and something pinching my wrist.

My eyes felt so heavy, like they were made of cement, and they refused to open. But I kept hearing Cal. I tried to move my hand where the pinch was coming from.

Finally, my eyes started to work, and I struggled to open them. I squinted, then tried to open them wide, which wasn't easy. The haze cleared a bit, and I saw Cal.

He was staring down at me, a look of pure terror on his face. 'Jesus Christ,' he said, and glanced at a watch in his hand.

I frowned and looked down to see the pinching was his fingers over the pulse in my wrist.

'What are you doing?' I asked in a groggy voice. My mouth felt dry, and the whole world was in slow motion.

'I'm taking your vitals,' he snapped, as if mad at me, which didn't make sense. I looked around. I was in his bed, still wearing his shirt. He was wearing pajama bottoms and a look of fear and anger.

He finally let go of my wrist, tossed the watch on the bedside table, and grabbed the glass of water that sat there.

'Here, drink this,' he helped me sit up. I took the water and drank, and he tucked the covers further around me like it was sixty below.

'What's wrong?' I asked, and set the cup back on the night stand.

He sat on the edge of the bed and looked at me. 'You wouldn't wake up,' he said with rage in his voice. 'You were freezing cold and didn't wake up. I physically tried moving you, anything, but you just ... were limp.' He shook his head and stood, grabbing the top of his head with both hands.

'I'm sorry. I took some sleeping pills last night because I couldn't sleep.'

His eyes shot to mine. 'How many?'

'Two. The bottle said—'

151

'Have you ever taken them before?'

'No, but I was so tired.'

'You should have started with *half* a pill. Damn it, Lana, you don't know how drugs will affect your system!'

He was so mad, but there was a rawness in his voice that made my heart break a little.

'I . . . I didn't know.' I'd followed the directions, but that didn't seem to matter. And, yes, they were new to me, but I thought it'd be okay, which it was. I was fine, they just apparently knocked me out into a deep sleep.

He scrubbed a hand down his face and muttered a string of curses.

'I didn't mean to frighten you,' I said quietly.

'Well, you did,' he snapped. 'I woke up, you had no covers on, your skin was like fucking ice, and I couldn't get you to open your eyes.'

I shook my head. The stupid drugs were still making things foggy, but I tried to put the pieces together. He was being kind of an ass, but he cared. I think. I shook my head again and squeezed my eyes shut, then opened them, desperate for this haze to clear.

'Why are you being mean?' I asked. At least, I was pretty sure he was being mean. I didn't know. I wasn't quite awake yet. I cupped my head in my palm.

'Shit,' Cal muttered, and came to sit next to me on the bed. He handed me the water again. 'I'm sorry,' he said. 'I didn't mean to yell.'

'You were taking my vitals?' I asked, sipping on the water.

He glanced away. But that was what he'd been doing. The fog was slowly clearing, and he'd been watching my heart rate. Which meant he had been worried.

'I really didn't know they'd knock me out like that,' I said.

'Okay.' He rose to stand again. I caught his arm.

'No, not okay. Why are you so mad at me?'

His eyes shot at me like two sparkling pools of clear water. 'You scared me. That's all. It's fine now.'

'No.' I tugged on his arm when he tried to walk away. 'It's not fine. I'm not fine. Tell me what is going on.'

'What's going on is I woke up thinking you were fucking dead.'

I gasped. 'Cal, that's . . . '

'Morbid? Yeah, tell me about it.'

Pieces started clicking. Bea had said his mother died of addiction. It was hard on Cal, but this? He was so young. Barely school aged.

'Did you see her use?' Something like that would mess with a child's mind.

'I saw her do a lot of things,' he said with disdain in his voice.

'It must have been hard when she passed—'

'She didn't pass,' he cut me off. 'She fucking died. Killed herself on accident because she couldn't handle her shit. And I found . . . '

My eyes shot wide, the final piece of the puzzle slipping into place.

'You were the one that found your mother dead?' I asked softly.

He tore his arm from my grip and walked away. Oh, my God. He did. I searched my memory for the conversation. Had Bea said he was six when Cal came to live with her? It would make sense, him being a child in the house and being the first one to find her. My chest instantly broke open for him.

'Cal?' I tried again, ambling up from the bed and following him into the living room. 'Cal, talk to me.'

He opened the fridge, then slammed it shut. Then he looked around the kitchen. He was lost. I saw it so clearly on his face, and he didn't know what to do.

'Talk to me,' I asked again softly. 'I scared you. Is it because you found your mom dead?'

'I didn't just *find* her.' He slapped one of the cabinets shut. 'I stayed with her. For a damn week!'

'What?'

He scoffed. 'She OD'd on the couch, and I couldn't figure out what was wrong with her. I knew she was cold. So I covered her in a blanket and sat with her. Talked to her. She didn't wake up.'

'Oh, my God.' A terrifying chill ran up my spine. I couldn't imagine what he'd gone through. How confusing and scary it was.

'Yep, I was a fucking idiot.'

'You were a child,' I said.

He just shook his head. He was getting lost in the pain. I recognized that kind of trauma. Something you thought out, constantly relived, but it never changed the outcome. It hurt to think about, yet when you did think about it, it consumed you. Then the questions came: What I could have done differently? What may have happened if only?

I didn't want Cal to get lost to those self-loathing feelings. Because there was no escape from the spiral once it started. This strong man ran from a lot of things, it was now I realized that he ran from the past as badly as I did. Trying not to think of the one moment when your life changed forever. It also made sense why he was such a protector the way he was.

I wanted to help. To bring him back to me. To the present.

So, I had to focus on the present.

'I didn't mean to scare you,' I said again. I took a step toward him. My bare feet hitting the cold hardwood of the kitchen floor.

'Go back to bed and get warm. Stay under the covers,' he ordered.

'Cal, I'm okay. Look at me.'

He finally met my eyes, so much pain and loss and fear were plaguing him, and all I wanted to do was make it better.

'I'm right here. And I'm okay.' I reached out for him, and he looked at my hand like it was a snake ready to bite. 'Please, baby,' I whispered. 'Come here.'

I wanted to hold him. Support him. The way he had done for me. There was so much beyond the surface of Callum Malone that I didn't even really know about yet. But I wanted to. I wanted to be what he needed now.

He finally took my hand, and I walked him back to bed. Keeping a tight hold, I laid down and brought him with me as I went. He resisted a little, but I kept pulling on his hand, and finally got him to lay with me – on top of me. Kicking the covers off, I wrapped my legs around his middle and my arms around his neck, and hugged him close.

'It's okay,' I whispered in his ear.

One of his strong arms wrapped around me, while the other cupped my face.

'Don't do that to me again,' he said.

'I won't. I didn't think they'd affect me like that.' I searched his face. 'Thank you for taking care of me.'

Though he was terrified, he'd stayed right there, in all his worry and still made sure I was okay. I couldn't imagine the stress and fear he'd gone through.

I kissed the side of his mouth, his cheek, and his jaw.

He turned and caught my mouth with his, kissing me deeply. But there was more this time. Fear and longing and relief.

He hugged me closer, like he was afraid I'd somehow disappear.

'I'm here,' I said. 'I'm right here.'

He kissed me hard and long. So much tension and aggression and concern. If I was thinking along different lines, it would almost feel loving.

He reached between us and pulled his pants down just enough to free his cock and bury it inside of me.

'Oh!' I moaned, loving the instant connection. He hugged me

tight, thrusting hard, but never retreating, simply staying deep and stirring. He was so big, so strong that I caught my breath every time he hugged me hard. But I loved the feel of being wrapped up in such power. Like he was holding on to me and silently promising me he wouldn't let me go.

He worked his body over mine. His lower torso rubbing over my clit while he moved so deeply already had me on the brink of coming.

I locked my ankles together and grabbed him as tightly as I could, taking everything. Hoping he'd give me everything, especially some of the burden he carried.

'Cal,' I whispered over and over. He just kissed me and rocked into my body like he was afraid to leave it.

'Lana . . .' he said my name and looked me in the eyes. With another powerful thrust, my orgasm burned slow, creeping up my spine and taking over my skin like thick lava. I couldn't breathe, didn't want to. I just gasped and watched him watch me. He kissed my lower lip, then gritted his teeth, and I felt his release shoot from him and carry my pleasure even higher.

Connected.

Holding each other so tight I didn't want to ever let go. Didn't want to be let go of.

And Cal was there, with all the mystery and pain and past that came with him. All things I wanted to know more about. I wanted to be what he needed. And I was afraid I might never understand the extent of his fear.

Chapter 16

The rest of week passed in a blur. Cal had been working several days, and I spent most of my time huddled inside my home. He didn't talk about his past any more. And I didn't push him. He'd told me what had happened, but how he dealt with it seemed to be a constant thing in his world. I only hoped he'd let me be a part of it. So far, he was. And I was thankful for that.

The shopping craze after Thanksgiving was finally subsiding, and I was making good progress on my classes and thesis. It was ever growing and changing, and my first meeting with my new advisor was now scheduled on Tuesdays, so I likely wouldn't run into Erica, and by proxy, Brock. I didn't know if that was done on purpose or not. But Professor Walker was a nice man in his late fifties. I had him for a class last year, so at least I was with someone I knew.

He had given me some good feedback, and we were going to meet one more time, really polish my proposal, then he would take it to the board after next week's meeting.

For now, I strolled down the streets of Golden, looked at the small shops, and tugged my scarf tighter around my neck. All the Christmas decorations were out, and things felt like holiday happiness. I still couldn't get Erica out of my mind. At some point, everything would come out, it always did. For now, I had no choice but to stay away.

I looked at a display of a sled with wrapped presents in the window and a reflection caught my eye. A man on the other side of the street with dark hair and a tall build caught my attention.

I turned around. He was on the other side of the street and further down in a black wool coat, perfect posture, and broad shoulders . . .

'Jack,' I whispered.

I went to walk across the street, but was cut off by a car. The man moved, walking down a side street and away from me. I wanted to call out. To have him stop.

It couldn't be him.

I couldn't tell, but my heart leapt into my throat with both hope and fear. When I finally made it across the street and down the alley, he'd gone. I caught myself thinking:

What if it was him?

What if it wasn't?

What would I say?

It didn't matter. Nothing registered. I just had to know if it was him. I hustled faster, but there was no one there. A small parking lot on the back side of the building was all I found. Not a soul in sight. Not a car that looked like it could be Jack's.

I closed my eyes and shook my head. I didn't know how to feel or what to think. This would happen. Unless Jack moved away forever, which wasn't the case since his family was here, I'd see him at some point.

The problem was, I just chased after what could have been him. To what end?

Hell if I knew.

I went after a shadow of what could have been my past. A past that had walked out on me. And then I decided to move – away from Jack and toward the man who would chase me to the ends of the earth. A man who had taken me to the edge of the world and didn't let go.

I made my way back toward Main Street and caught the smell of the local coffee shop. I wondered if they served spiked peppermint mochas this time in the afternoon.

I stirred the dip, which was sour cream and an onion soup packet, about the extent of my 'cooking skills,' and balanced the phone between my ear and shoulder.

'So, you're having a good time?' I asked Harper.

'Yeah, family is crazy, but it's good.' Harper had a handful of brothers and sisters, and parents that were still together. Everyone was loud and nosy, but it all came from a place of love. I could hear everyone chatting in the background. I was glad I'd stayed behind, because while Harper's family was wonderful, they all had their own lives, and I wasn't really a part of it.

'I miss you,' she said.

'I miss you too.'

'How are things going with Cal?'

I breathed deep. 'Pretty well. I like him. A lot. He's ... different.'

'Different good or different than Jack?'

Of course, Harper wouldn't miss that. 'Both.'

The last few weeks, I'd seen differences and similarities and realized that Bea was right, they picked up the slack in the areas the other one lacked.

'I wanted to check in because I've been working remotely. I may stay here for another few weeks until after Christmas.'

'Oh!' I said, pausing mid-stir.

'Will you be okay with me gone that long?'

I thought about that. I'd been without Harper before, a week here and there, but this was already extended. Still, she had a life and a family.

'Of course, I'm fine. You have a great time and enjoy your family.'

'Call if you need anything.'

'Thanks.'

We hung up and I grabbed a bag of chips and set it next to the dip. That was my contribution to tonight. A night I was a little nervous about, actually.

I checked the mirror one more time, my sweater and jeans still in place. Make-up was good. Now, I just waited. Cal would be here any minute and yet, I stared at my phone and did the one thing I shouldn't.

I dialed my dad.

After seeing him before Thanksgiving, he'd been plaguing my thoughts more. It was sick, but I wondered how he was. If he was okay. He'd made it clear for me to stay away. For whatever reason, I wanted to hear his voice. Because the one moment we had, where he'd acknowledged there was a life before Anita, before Brock, pinged my chest and it wouldn't subside.

When I got his voicemail for the hundredth time in months, it was no surprise, yet the sting of realizing he didn't want to talk to me hurt.

But for the first time in a long time, I left a message.

'Hey, Dad. I just wanted to say . . . lots of things, actually. But mostly that you're my dad.' I shrugged as if he could see me. Because it was that simple. It hurt, it didn't make sense, and I was so angry with him. Didn't trust him. He didn't want me. And yet, 'You're my dad.' I whispered and glanced down. 'Okay, bye.'

Probably the world's worst voicemail, but it was better than nothing. Because, despite the past, I was insane when it came to my father. I'd keep trying to reach him for the rest of my life. Knowing he wouldn't reach back. There was no logical reason for it other than he was my father.

A knock came at the door and I opened it to find Cal looking amazing, as usual. He was in his standard blue fire T-shirt and matching pants. The casual uniform.

'It's cold out, you know,' I said.

'I told you, I run hot, and we're just walking across the street.' I grabbed the dip. 'Aw, Kitten, you cooked.'

'I stirred. It's chips and dip.'

'The guys will love it.'

The firemen, apparently, had a group dinner every night at around six. And tonight, I was invited.

'You look nervous?'

'I am!'

He smiled. 'Don't be. We have guests all the time, and the guys have already met you.'

Yeah, but Rhett and I had an unspoken secret of sorts when he caught me at the station leaving Cal's room. I didn't want to turn into the department joke. And having Cal's friends and crew like me was very important.

'This is a regular thing we do. Just dinner and bullshit. Don't let them rile you, and you'll be fine.'

Somehow, that didn't help at all. 'Don't let them rile me?'

Cal shrugged. 'I'm bringing a chick over. They will give me shit.'

'Why? Like you said, I've been over a couple times.'

'Which makes them give me more shit. That's how we work. And because I've never brought a girl over. '

'That's not true,' I mumbled, thinking of what Rhett had said about it not being uncommon for Cal to have ladies come and go from his room.

'What did you say?'

I just shook my head. Now wasn't the time, and it didn't matter anyway. He could do what he wanted. I had slept with his best

161

friend, for goodness sakes, so I really couldn't be jealous. Yet, part of me wondered what Cal's routine with women was.

'Alright then, let's head over.'

He grabbed the chips, kissed me quick, then took my hand in his free one and led me across the street. Weaving through the station's living quarters, we rounded the corner to another hallway, and there was a large open kitchen. A long island was in the middle and had a ton of food set out on it. A circular table that could easily fit twelve people was the focal point of the room. Able and Rhett were grilling something on the stove, while Mark and Dave set the table.

'Wow,' I said. They moved like a unit. A family.

'Yeah, dinnertime is sort of our thing. We all sit down together and try to be civil for an hour.' Cal winked at me, then said, 'I think you've caught a glimpse of this area, but over here is where we hang out.'

A few more steps down the hall, and there was the living room with two large couches, along with four recliners that made a semi-circle around the massive big screen TV hanging on the wall. It was all open and made for guys. One thing I hadn't noticed before was the pole in the corner.

'I didn't know firehouses still came with a pole, even if it's a single story.'

'They don't. This came from when this place was older, we remodeled a while back and kept the pole. It still serves a purpose.' His tone was playful, and his hand slid to my ass.

'I bet it does.'

'Any time you feel the need to express yourself, say, spinning around, feel free to use the pole, Kitten.'

'I'll keep that in mind.'

He gave me a little smack on the butt and kissed me quick. 'That about completes the grand tour, since you've seen where the trucks are and my room.'

I nodded and we headed back to the kitchen. Cal put the chips and dip on the counter next to the other food that was brought.

'Hey, man,' Able said, wearing the same Golden Fire T-shirt. They were all dressed the same. All on duty. There were two other women there, which I wasn't prepared for, but happy I wasn't the only one.

'Hey,' Cal said to his buddy. 'You remember, Lana.'

'Of course, we've been hearing lots about you,' he said. He pointed the large tongs at Cal. 'This guy over here talks in his sleep, and I swear to God, if he calls out your name one more time—'

'Shut up,' Cal said, and flicked a piece of salad at Able.

'No, it's Cal here won't shut up about you,' Able continued. Cal just gave him a 'piss off' look, and Able chuckled and motioned for one of the women to come over. A tall blond approached. 'This is my wife, Stephanie.'

'Nice to meet you,' I said to the woman.

'You too. Do you want some cider?' she offered.

'That would be great, thanks.' I walked with her to the table where a plethora of drinks were laid out. The guys couldn't drink alcohol, obviously, but they had everything from Gatorade to sparkling blueberry fiber water. There were also a couple juice boxes.

I glanced at Cal and laughed at the spread. It was adorable. He just shrugged, and then continued chatting with Able. Every so often, he glanced over his shoulder and tossed me a wink.

'So, when is the big day?' Stephanie asked, pouring two fresh cups of cider.

Confusion hit me. 'Big day for what?'

She looked at me, surprised, then at my left hand, then back at me. 'Oh, are you and Cal not engaged?'

Shock took over confusion real quick and a nervous laugh

escaped. I felt horrible. Not because the idea of being married to guy like Cal wasn't a good one, it was just not even close to where we were in our relationship.

'No, we're just dating,' I said hesitantly. Partly because the word sounded both too presumptuous and too tame at the same time. What we did, how I felt, went way beyond 'dating,' yet the complications that came with our situation made it seem like a pushy step forward.

'Oh, sorry,' she said. 'I just thought that wives and fiancés were the only ones to come to these things.'

I looked around. It was just me, Stephanie and another woman who had a ring on her finger and was hovering near Dave. Dave's wife then?

'I thought these dinners were casual and happened all the time?'

'They do. I'm so sorry,' she said again, and handed me a mug. 'You are more than welcome. It was my mistake to assume. Obviously, you're very important to Cal. Who needs labels, right?'

Her sunny smile was welcome, but she was backpedaling. Still, I appreciated her trying to make me feel better. The more I looked on, the more I saw just how this group of people functioned.

Like a family.

Everyone knew everyone, and they were all laughing and exchanging stories. This was Cal's world. A big part of it, and I was on the outside. But part of me so desperately wanted to be more. Closer to him. A part of his world.

I had a shot with Bea. I felt comfortable with her and loved being a part of her home. But maybe this aspect of Cal's life I didn't fit well into. I just stood there, not knowing how to interact or what to do. I was awkward and looking in on something I didn't fully understand.

'Here, come meet Trish,' Stephanie said, and hustled me to

where Trish was standing. She introduced me. Dave was the first to say something, though.

'Lana! It's good to see you back.'

'So, Cal is yours, huh?' the pretty redhead asked. She reminded me of Harper. Dave just shook his head. 'My wife loves gossip.'

'Do not,' she argued. 'Okay, I totally do,' she said with a smile. 'And Cal is great, so I'm excited to see him finally bring one of you around.'

My face fell, and Dave muttered a curse.

'Oh, that's not what I meant. I'm so sorry. That came out really, really wrong.'

'It's okay,' I said lowly, trying to take the words, 'one of you around,' out of my head. Apparently, everyone knew about Cal's tastes and lack of commitment. I was starting to feel more like that joke I didn't want to be. It also made sense now what Cal had said. He hadn't brought a girl around. What he meant was, he never brought them around his crew.

'Lana here went up in the ladder,' Dave said, trying to change the subject. He was really a sweet man.

'Wow,' Trish said. 'I can't get on that thing. I'm way too scared.'

'Nah, Lana was a champ,' Dave said. His easy personality and happy demeanor made me feel better. Then, his eyes shifted to the grill. 'Rhett, have you said hi to Lana?'

Rhett just nodded and waved, but didn't say anything.

'Don't mind him,' Dave said. 'He's been pissy lately, and none of us knows why.'

Funny, my best friend had been pissy lately too, and last time I saw her she was getting a snack with Rhett after our run. Something was going on with him and Harper, it had to be.

'So, tell us how you and Cal met?' Stephanie asked.

All the eyes turned to me. A shiver of nervousness rose, but they all looked nice and eager to know.

'He literally swept me off my feet last summer.'

'Oh, yeah!' Trish said. 'The race in the park after the barbecue.'

'I love that race. Able flips me around, and every time makes me feel like a princess he's carrying through the woods.'

I smiled because, yeah, that was what it felt like. These women could relate, and I realized then that while I may be new to this, I could relate too. Because Cal was amazing, a protector, and at every turn tried to make me a part of his world.

His past, both with women and even further back, was appearing to be trickier than I'd imagined. But the truth remained that Cal hadn't lied to me. He hadn't sold me on anything other than what he was.

Whether it was at the barbecue when I first met him, taking me to his aunt's, or even now, he was actually letting me in. Something I wasn't used to, but craving more and more of.

'I have to admit that I'm glad you're the one who finally got Cal to settle down. Bets were starting to go around about whether he'd be a bachelor for life,' Stephanie said in a low tone.

Trish nodded in agreement.

'I heard he wasn't really into commitment,' I said.

They both laughed. 'We've never seen a woman actually with him. Because he never brought any of them to any events. You must be pretty special.'

I sipped my cider and glanced at Cal again. He smiled back. There was a warmth behind his eyes that made me melt.

'I am lucky,' I said, and I meant it. Because I wasn't just lucky, I was falling hard for the man that seemed to have a way with picking me up and carrying me when I needed him the most.

Chapter 17

Chirp.

'What is that noise?' Cal asked, walking into my house.

'It's the alarm. It's been randomly chirping.'

Cal frowned at the control unit on the wall and hit a few buttons, then locked the dead bolt.

'Probably doesn't help you sleep,' he said.

'Yeah, it's annoying. I was going to call the alarm company tomorrow.'

'Yeah, do that. Just to see why it's glitching.'

He followed me toward my room. 'You alright? You've been quiet.'

I folded my lips together. I didn't know what to say. The women were nice, the crew was on their best behavior, from what I could tell. And yet, the thought of women going in and out stuck in my mind.

I wasn't a secret. Cal wasn't keeping me a secret. And I trusted him. So the comments made about him finally 'settling down,' rocked me in different ways. I was realizing how much of a 'ladies man' he was, and also wondering, if I was the reason he was 'settling down.'

Lots of thoughts. But nothing I wanted to go into. Things would continue to grow and morph how they would. It was nice being a part of the dinner, though.

'I'm fine. Tonight was fun,' I said, and I kicked off my boots by my bed. 'The girls are really nice.'

'Yeah, they are,' Cal said, and pulled his shirt off. I instantly stilled, hypnotized by his amazing chest and abs, and my mouth salivated like Pavlov's damn dog.

Cal chuckled. 'You want a taste? All you have to do is come and get it, Kitten.'

'I just may.'

Everything about him, about us, in this moment was so . . . simple. Like a couple getting ready for bed together was a normal thing. Like we could be happy and not have all these past issues hanging over our heads.

I thought about Jack and how I thought I'd seen him. Then I looked at Cal. I knew, right then, that this was where I wanted to be. Not chasing a shadow. But with Cal.

'Um . . . Stephanie said that usually fiancés are the ones to show up to these dinners.'

'That's generally true.'

'But you brought me?'

'You're important to me.' He crawled across the bed, then sat in front of me and pulled me to stand between his spread legs. Looking up at me, he cupped my hips, this thumbs running beneath my sweater and along my stomach. 'You're *very* important to me.'

'You're important to me too.'

He lifted my sweater just enough to place a kiss on my bellybutton. I gently ran my fingers through his hair. The endearment was so delicate, so sensitive, that it made water come to my eyes for some reason.

'It's like there's another word I could use to fully describe how I feel . . .' he rasped against my skin, his lips trailing along my stomach.

168

My gaze shot down. He couldn't mean what I thought, could he?

'Another word?' I asked.

He nodded, delivering another kiss.

'I'm in—'

'Crazy?' I asked quickly. Because this was crazy. If he was going to say what it sounded like, I . . . I didn't know what to say back. But my heart beat faster and, while I wanted to hear it, wanted it to be true, I was terrified. It was too soon, wasn't it? There was too much between us, too much we'd have to deal with, like other people, and the past, and . . . .

With deep emotion in his eyes and said, 'Yes, I'm in crazy with you.'

He was serious. He switched 'love' out with the word I gave him, but he meant it, and I felt it. And I wanted it. And him. With everything I was. Everything that was left of me, I was ready to give him.

I should know better.

I did know better.

But the man holding me, actively making me a part of his every day and his life was the one I trusted.

'Cal,' I whispered, and that water behind my eyes rose further to the surface. 'I'm in crazy with you too.'

A smile lit his face and he instantly rose, cupped my neck, and pulled me in for a searing kiss. I didn't have time to think or do anything, I just got lost in his kiss and his touch. He maneuvered me onto the bed and laid me on my back, his mouth never leaving mine. Instead, it explored and skimmed along my skin as he removed my sweater, then my jeans.

Kissing my thighs, my knees, down to my ankles and back.

'Cal,' I whispered his name and ran my hand through his hair. He rested his chin on my hip. The way his blue eyes sparkled and the position were so intimate, yet so casual, my love looking up at me while his stubble scratched my skin as he smiled.

'I'm here, love,' he said, kissing my stomach as he hooked his fingers into my panties and slowly peeled them down my legs and off.

He ran his nose up my knee, to my inner thigh, then sucked the fleshy part into his mouth. I felt so alive. So loved. So seen.

He trailed his lips up my ribs, unsnapping my bra and gently licking along my breast thoroughly before taking the nipple in. He sucked slowly, laving attention on my body and skin so much that I felt like a queen. Worshiped and happy and relaxed.

Lying next to me, he kissed my neck and kicked his jeans down and off. Finally, I felt his hot skin brush against mine. His cock nudged my side, but he didn't make any move to cover me or enter. He just stayed off to the side, kissing along my throat while his big hand cupped my face, then trailed lower to my core.

When his fingers found my clit, I jolted a little, but his lips were right there to catch my gasp as he started rubbing. I reached out and grabbed his hard cock in my fist to hang on as he worked me over.

He just kept rubbing, slow and intent, while he kissed the corner of my mouth and my jaw, taking my breath with his. As I shuddered out an exhale, he'd breathe it in. So in sync. I wanted more. Wanted to be wrapped up in him.

I wiggled, keeping tight hold of his cock, and tried to line us up. He just kept rubbing, my orgasm climbing and climbing.

His eyes stayed on my face. Stayed right there with me. I was so close and felt so empty at the same time.

His free hand slid under my back and wrapped around me, cupping my breast and pulling me close so that I shifted enough for my bottom to line up with his hips and my back pressed against his chest. I threw my leg over his, opening myself more to him.

He just kept rubbing.

Over and over, the heat was so intense, the tremors taking over my body were slowly burning me up. With my back against his chest and both of us on our sides, I was spread wide for his hand, his cock running along my thigh, so close to where I needed him.

'Please,' I begged on a whisper. 'I'm going . . .'

'Crazy?' he rasped.

'Yes.' His hold tightened on me and I was done for. I was crazy about Cal. Crazy in love with him.

Right when his hand picked up speed, bringing my release to the surface, he moved just enough to slip the head of his cock into me. I couldn't hold back. I came hard, with just the crown inside me and his hand working me over.

'I'll never get tired of feeling you come on me,' he rasped, and sank a little deeper, pushing through my contracting inner walls and throwing me into a pleasure spiral I could barely handle. 'Keep coming for me. I want you drenched, Kitten. Because you are the one who makes me crazy.'

He thrust to the hilt and I gasped, my muscles relaxing because, finally, he was inside me completely. A part of me.

Keeping his hand on my mound, he spread two fingers like a V so that he could feel his cock slide in and out of me with every thrust. All the while, his other strong arm held me captive. Fucking me from behind, yet wrapping me up all at the same time.

I looked down to see where we joined. Watching him disappear inside of me over and over was enough to make me come again. But I wanted to see his face first. Feel his pleasure. In a different way than ever before.

'I want to see you come, baby,' I whispered.

I turned my head so I could see the side of his face. He looked at me and I ran a hand over his, over where we were joined, then up to my stomach and breast. 'Let me see it?'

'Anything you want,' he rasped and fucked me harder. Though the moment was beyond intense and loving, it was hard and fast. He was in total control of my body. Feeling everything, watching everything.

I reached behind me and cupped his head. He kissed along my neck then bit down gently just as he pulled out of my body, his heavy cock rested against my core and he came hard. His release lashing my skin like a hot brand along my stomach.

His breaths were rough and fast. He kissed my shoulder, neck, and ear. I just cupped his head and kept him close. Then he did something unexpected, he grabbed his still hard, pulsing cock and slipped back inside me.

'Oh, God!' I jolted.

He stirred deep and the orgasm that had been brewing shot to life and overtook me.

'Fucking incredible,' he growled in my ear. 'Watching you come apart while marked by me.' He gripped around my breasts tighter. 'You're mine, Lana,' he said with so much command it made me shudder. I'd never heard him so dominating before. I liked it. It also reminded me that there was something very demanding and deep hidden in Cal. Something very primal that went with his protectiveness.

My body gently shook as we clung to each other. I felt free and totally confined at the same time.

'You're mine,' he whispered again.

The only thing I could say was the truth. 'Yes. I'm yours.'

Chapter 18

'Come here, Kitten,' Cal said, holding out his hand. He was gloriously naked and standing by the steaming shower, waiting for me.

Taking his hand, he guided me beneath the spray of the water and joined me. The water washed away my tired muscles and the evidence of our lovemaking from just moments ago.

He grabbed my shampoo, squirted some into his hands, and massaged my scalp.

'Wow, this is quite the treatment,' I said with closed eyes, loving the relaxation his fingers worked into my head.

'I'm a full service kind of guy,' he said, and I could hear his grin.

'Yes, you are.'

He gently pinched my nipple, and I jumped.

Anchoring me under the spray again, he rinsed my hair, and followed with conditioner. Facing him, he ran his fingers through my hair and up high until the wet strands dropped from his fingers and slapped my back.

'Are you . . . playing?'

'Yeah,' he said unapologetically, combing his fingers through my hair again, lifting his arms high until . . .

Slap, slap, slap, the wet locks came down. I couldn't really complain because watching his impressive body stretch and all those ab muscles flex was a mighty fine sight.

'Well then, I suppose I should get busy with you then.'

'I like the sound of that.'

Holy crap, his cock was already stirring and semi-hard. The man was a machine. I grabbed my loofah. 'I meant wash you. Good Lord, are you ever satisfied?' I asked, glancing down at his, yep, definitely growing, erection.

'With you? I'm insatiable.'

He kissed me quickly and continued playing with my hair. The act was so comfortable. Just tra la la, taking a shower, no big deal, totally naked with the man I—

Loved.

I glanced at his face and started slow circles over his chest with the bubbly loofah. I loved Cal. Somehow when I wasn't supposed to. Somehow throughout the pain and broken ache in my chest, the last half of my soul left reached out for him, and loved him. I may have thought there were similarities between him and Jack, I knew there were just as many, if not more, differences.

Yet one thing stood out:

'You said I was yours,' I whispered, concentrating on my task of washing him. His hands on me stilled.

'Yes.'

'What does that mean . . . how does that work?' I'd been down this road with Jack. Everything was left up to his control, for the most part. I was along for the ride and took what I could, and grew and learned, but in the end, I was on his time.

Now, Cal was staking a claim, the same one Jack had once made. It forced the leftover bits of my heart to hurt a little.

'Honestly, I don't know how all of this is going to work,' he said. Gently taking the loofah from me, he started gently washing my chest, breasts, and down to my stomach. 'There will be realities we can't avoid.'

'Like Jack,' I said.

'Yes, like Jack.' Cal didn't sound confident in that, but he also didn't sound deterred. He sounded almost prepared. Like, whenever Jack showed up, he'd be ready.

'What I feel and what is actually possible are pulling at each other.'

'What do you feel?'

We'd alluded to this earlier, but time to come out and say it.

'I love you,' I said, and met his stare. 'To be honest, that was easier than trusting you. But I do. I know better, I've been hurt and I won't lie to you . . . but I don't know if I'll ever be the same. Jack changed something in me. Took a piece of me with him.' I closed my eyes and tried to gather myself before the sting behind my eyes hurt too badly. 'But I trust you, so much. And somewhere in that, I fell in love with you too.'

Cal's brows sliced down and he looked at me like he was both shocked and angry? Did I upset him by talking about Jack?

'I just wanted to be honest with you,' I started quickly, defending my words, but he cut me off.

'I always want you to be honest with me. I know your feelings about Jack and the struggle.' He dropped the loofah and cupped my face. 'I'm just glad you have some room left for me.'

I blinked several times. How could be so understanding? It hit me then that Cal knew what to expect and was the calm before the storm. A storm Jack would bring with him. A storm we'd have to face at some point. A storm I'd have to weather.

'Hey, hey, don't look so sad,' he said. 'Listen to me carefully. This moment, right now, is what I'm going to hold on to. Whatever happens, however we deal with it, right now is what I'm betting on. Okay?'

I nodded. 'Okay,' I whispered.

He kissed me, and both of us went under the spray just as tears fell from my eyes. I squeezed them shut and wrapped my arms around Cal. He lifted me up and I wrapped my legs around his waist. He fastened me to his cock like I was meant to be there, like he was meant to be inside of me.

I moaned and just kissed him, staying still and reveling in the feeling of him simply inside me. A part of me. A few quick turns of the knobs and the shower was off, and Cal was walking us back to bed. He sat down with me in his lap and our wet skin sliding against each other's. I just kissed him and kissed him, afraid to let him go. Afraid he'd take back his words, his claim. Afraid of the future and what it held.

Afraid that I wouldn't know what to do when it came.

Chapter 19

I choked out a sob and shot up in bed. Breathing hard and trying to clear the fog from my sleepy eyes, I looked around my bedroom. Dark. But I wasn't alone. Cal was next to me, sitting up, his blue eyes fused to mine. I reached for him. 'I'm sorry, I must have been having a nightmare.'

'Don't be sorry. Are you okay? You were mumbling in your sleep,' he said in a low voice.

'Yeah.' I took another breath and grabbed his bicep, as if I physically needed to feel his support. I couldn't remember what I was dreaming of, but I knew I was scared.

A creak came from the front room.

'Shhh.' Cal put up his hand, and in a fast, silent action, got out of bed and put on his jeans.

Another creak sounded.

He leaned over onto to the bed, his face an inch from mine, and cupped my jaw. 'There's someone in the house.' My blood instantly flooded my brain, and fear shot through every vein, as I tensed to run. Cal gripped me. 'Do you have a phone in here?' he whispered quietly.

'No.' My cell was out in the front room, and judging by the look on Cal's face, he didn't have his either.

He grabbed his shirt and pulled it over my head. 'You're going to hide in that corner,' he pointed to the one next to the window.

'The second I leave this room, you go out that window and run to the firehouse. Do you understand?'

I shook my head wildly. 'No, no you can't—'

'I will take care of the person in the house, you run. I won't let him come after you or hurt you.' With that, he left me, and quietly and shut the bedroom door behind him.

No! No, this wasn't happening. I was terrified. Someone was in my home, and I had a pretty good idea who it was. Brock. He wouldn't leave me alone. He never would.

I heard a crash of something breaking, and then the front door slammed.

'Cal!' I screamed, and ran into the front room. The vase was broken in the kitchen, and I looked around in the dark, but saw no one. Flipping on the light, I screamed for Cal again. Screeching tires from down the street sounded, and I ran to the front door and opened it. Cal was hustling back toward me, barefoot and shirtless.

'What the hell are you doing?' he barked. 'I told you to run.'

I threw myself into his arms and hugged him tight. He caught me and hugged me back.

'Are you okay?' I whispered.

'Yeah, Kitten. Are you?' He set me back to look at me.

'Yeah, I'm fine. What happened? Who was it?'

He took my hand and brought me inside, locked my door, and sat me on the couch with a blanket. Picking up my cell, he called the police.

'I didn't make out who the person was. It looks like they got in with no force. Does anyone have a key?'

'No, no one except Harper and me.'

Cal scrubbed a hand down his face. 'He had someone waiting in the car. It was a silver 4×4. I couldn't make out the plate, but he got away. He had help.'

'Was it Brock?'

'I can't be sure.'

I closed my eyes, and the blue and red started flashing, followed by a knock at the door. The police.

'Why?' I asked.

Cal cupped my face. 'I don't know. But I'm going to keep you safe. Whether they were looking for you, or just house burglars, this won't happen again.'

'This isn't your fault,' I said.

'I disarmed the alarm.'

'But the doors were locked.'

'I should have known better.' He shook his head. 'You're not leaving my sight.'

Just then, the police officers came in and Cal started talking to one of them while the other spoke with me, recapping what happened.

'Do you know of anyone who'd want to break in or hurt you, Miss Case?' the officer asked.

Yes, I did. But they couldn't help me beat him.

'They were looking for something,' I said to Aunt Bea, who handed me a cup of tea and sat right next to me on her couch. 'The police don't know what it was, but all my books and the small desk in the corner of the living room were messed up.'

'Did they take anything?' she asked.

I shook my head. 'Not that I can tell.'

'Thank God you were there, Cal,' Bea said, looking at her nephew, who was pacing the floor. It had been a long night. By the time we wrapped things up with the police, it was dawn. Cal had packed me a bag and brought me straight here.

'I disarmed the alarm,' he mumbled. 'So, it was actually bad I was there.'

'You heard what the police said,' I defended. 'Some people will mess with alarms to get them to chirp so they get turned off. I would have done it eventually.'

'That also means someone is watching you and waiting.' He shook his head. 'It's that fucker step-brother of yours.'

Yeah, I thought that too. Problem was, we had no evidence, and we both knew it. Someone has been messing with me for a while. I'd thought someone had been in my home a couple months back. But what did they want? If it was Brock, looking to hurt me, wouldn't he have come straight to my room?

I shook my head.

'He wants something.' I just didn't know what. 'Or he's just trying to keep me scared.' Which he was doing a bang up job of at the moment. I was scared. But also mad. Not to mention, Cal had been a ball of fury for the past twelve hours.

He looked at his watch. 'Shit, I've got two on, so for the next forty-eight hours, you're staying here,' he said to me.

'Yes, I already made up the guest room,' Bea agreed.

'Thank you.' Normally, I wouldn't want to be scared out of my home, but Cal was furious. I was actually scared, and didn't want to be alone. Especially when I had a feeling this mess ran deeper than I was aware of.

I followed Cal out to his truck, and before he opened the door, I grabbed his hand.

'I'm sorry I didn't listen to you and go out the window like you said.'

'My concern right now is you and your safety.'

'I appreciate what you did and . . . ' I looked at him. 'I ran after you because it was just instinct.'

He cupped my face and kissed me softly. 'Yes.' Another soft kiss. 'Don't ever do that again.'

He got in his truck and pulled away. Forty-eight hours. I had class and was staying with Bea. In the meantime, I needed to focus on what the hell was happening in my life. And why someone insisted on messing with me.

Chapter 20

It was late, and after helping Bea clean up from dinner, we sat in the living room. The same brown shag carpet stretched the entire length of the house, and the small coffee table in the middle of the room had a couple chips and dings on it. I looked closer, it also had what appeared to be crayon and marker. This house probably looked exactly how it did when Cal was growing up. And that thought comforted me.

'You want to talk, honey? Today must be weighing on you.'

I nodded, loving that she was so supportive and took time to chat with me.

'It's more than that.' I had my final meeting with my advisor tomorrow to take my thesis proposal to the board for approval. Then the real work would begin. Not to mention Cal and Jack, and my brain was not cooperating.

I just kept replaying those three words in my mind: *You are mine.*

They both had said them to me.

'It's funny, a couple months ago, I would have been paralyzed with fear right now over what happened. I mean, I'm scared,' I said, 'But I'm dealing with it.'

'That's a good thing. You've grown.'

'I've grown because Jack helped me do that. But he's gone. I'm not the same in good and bad ways because he left.'

Bea nodded. 'Jack needs certain things in his life to function. Like control. But he's also loyal to a fault. He would do anything for people he loves.'

I hung my head. I wasn't one of those people. Cal and Bea were, I hadn't been. The pain still stabbed, but there was nothing I could do. And I was happy with Cal.

'I love Cal,' I admitted, and Bea smiled.

'I know, honey.'

'But what if I can't get Jack's shadow out of my system?'

'Jack's presence is a powerful one. That's what happens when someone affects your life, both in good and bad ways. They linger.'

'I feel like I'm betraying Cal.'

'No, honey, you're dealing with emotions that are strong. The boys know what they got themselves into with you.'

'What do you mean?'

Bea just looked at me with a little shock and then softness. Softness that resembled pity. 'They're like brothers, honey,' she said, like I wasn't aware of how close they were. 'Just because Jack isn't in Denver doesn't mean that stops.'

Cal admitted that Jack already knew about us. But it didn't occur to me that they spoke regularly. 'So, you think Jack and Cal talk a lot?'

'I know that those two boys are thick and have never kept secrets from each other. I also know they wouldn't hurt each other, or you.'

And yet, Jack left. But Bea's admission shouldn't shock me. Of course they would talk. I wasn't a part of any of that, and probably for a good reason. I told Cal once that I didn't want to know.

'I don't know all the details. The boys have had their own language since they were kids that I just don't understand, but what I do know is that you're in the middle.'

My lips parted because so much concern plagued her face. 'They've gone through some tough times together, but you're the only thing I've been truly worried about.'

'Worried?' I asked.

She nodded. 'Honey, you're the only thing powerful enough to wreck them both.'

I gasped. 'That ... no, I wouldn't—'

'I know you wouldn't. But it doesn't mean that's not how it will end up.'

'But Jack left. He wrecked me.'

I hated sounding like I was pleading my own case, but I had no choice. It was the first time I'd really talked out loud about details and remembered the way Jack looked at me before he turned his back.

'I fought for him,' I said, water lining my voice. 'And he walked.'

'I know, honey.' She pulled me into a hug. 'I know. But don't think Jack walked away without some scratches too.'

'It doesn't matter. I love Cal, and I just want ... ' Bea leaned back and looked at me. 'I want to say I wish I'd never met Jack. That I want everything but Cal and me to go away. All the experiences and time and pain and—'

'Love?'

I nodded. Loving Jack was so different than loving Cal. They each brought out something different. Maybe Cal had been right. Maybe it was better that things had happened the way they did and I'd met Jack how I did. Because it made me who I was. Made me able to love Cal the way I did.

'Why is this so hard?'

'Men always are,' she said. 'What you need to worry about now is you. Getting that degree you're so excited about and keeping safe.'

184

'Yeah, you're right.'

'What do your parents say about all this?'

'My parents aren't really around. Well, my dad lives here in Denver, but we don't talk. Actually, he wants nothing to do with me.'

'Why? Cal mentioned your step-brother being a piece of work who was vicious to you as a child, but surely your father—'

'My dad hasn't really ever backed me since he married Anita. Even now, he treats Brock more like his kid than me. Which is fine. I learned my lesson.'

'It's not fine,' Bea said softly. 'I'm sorry you've had such disappointment in your life. But your parent is supposed to be the one person you can count on.'

'Maybe that's why I connected with Cal and Jack the way I did.'

Bea nodded. 'Yes, they've had their share of disappointment.'

'Cal told me some . . .' I said slowly.

'Both the boys had a tough time. Cal, for a few years, didn't talk. Kept to himself. Finally started to open up when he was eight. Staying with his mother like he did hurt him in a way that worries me to this day.' She shook her head. 'I hate my sister so much for leaving him like that. Somewhere deep down, I think he still blames himself. Like he could have saved her.'

Tears flooded my eyes. I couldn't imagine Cal as a young child staying with his dead mother, trying to take care of her, only for her to never wake up.

'You've taken such good care of him,' I told Bea.

'No, honey, you take care of him. He's been outrunning bad memories for a long time. But, you came along, and I've never seen him act like this before. Part of me thought he was running into a fire just to feel himself burn, but you've brought him back.'

It all made sense. Why he was so protective. Why he was scared when I was in danger. He needed control in his own way. Only his way was living fast and hard on the edge, and once his feet stopped moving, the stillness and reality of what could go wrong scared him.

'Jackie helped so much. They became fast friends when Jack and his dad moved across the street. Jack was here more than his own home.'

I nodded. 'Jack told me once that Cal saved him from hurting his dad?'

Bea nodded. 'They were teenagers. One night, that horrible man was beating up on Jackie, and I started to go over, but Cal stopped me and went himself. Only, he got there and found Jack was the one beating his father. He'd fought back, and Cal pulled him off before ...'

I knew the rest, but poor Bea couldn't say it. Jack had almost beat his father to death. I remembered the look in his dark eyes when he'd told me. Told me how he didn't understand love without some kind of pain. He owed Cal his whole life because, if his father had died, Jack would have been lost.

'They really are brothers,' I whispered. They had been through so much together. 'I'm so glad they have you.'

Bea smiled. 'I'm glad they have you too, honey.'

I wanted to say that they didn't have me. Cal did. But I didn't want to ruin her moment. She was like their mother and loved them, and I didn't want to ruin that.

'There's something special about you,' Bea said. 'Anyone who can't see it is blind or stupid.'

She was so warm and kind and ... motherly. Something in my chest that I didn't know was missing started filling the day I met Bea. Something like a sense of family and having a parent in your corner.

She wasn't my parent. I knew that. But mine didn't give a shit, and there was something so magnetic about her that made me just wanted to be a part of this family unit so badly. She loved Jack and Cal, defended them and took care of them. What that must feel like to have someone care for you in that way. The way a parent probably should.

'Thank you so much,' I said.

One tear managed to escape.

Chapter 21

'Okee-dokie, Miss Case, let's get this proposal to the thesis board,' Mr. Walker said, while chewing on a bagel. His office was dark, no window, and cluttered in a way that made me itch to call *Hoarders* to come in and do a TV special. But he was nice and competent. He was also brilliant in his scattered ways.

I let out a deep breath and resisted the urge to jump up and down. Yes, I still had some classes to take, and more to write up on this thesis, but once it was approved, I could really take off with it.

'You should let Erica know. She was sorry to lose you as a student,' Mr. Walker said.

I snapped my attention to him. 'What?'

'You know.' He waved the half-eaten bagel around. 'With family obligations and whatnot, I know she was sad to have to lose you.'

I didn't think Erica would have said anything overly negative. In fact, the school likely wouldn't have to know of the conflict of interest with her engagement to my step-brother, but I didn't know she'd said anything to Mr. Walker about me or the situation.

'I was sorry to lose her too. Not to say working with you hasn't been great.'

'Of course. All the students like me. I always have jellybeans,' he said with so much pride and opened his first desk drawer. 'Hmmm.' Then he opened his second desk drawer. 'They're around here somewhere,' he mumbled.

'That's okay, Mr. Walker, I'll get some jellybeans next time.'

'Okay then. Well, if you want me to pass on the good news of going to the board to Erica, I certainly can next time I see her.'

'Is she not around as much?' I asked.

'She's been trying to cut back a little to have more time with her daughter.'

'Wait,' I said quickly. 'She has a daughter?'

He nodded. 'Yeah, she's going through a rough time at school, I believe, and she's been needing her mom more lately, it sounds like.'

'How old is she?' I asked with horror in my voice.

'Twelve or thirteen, I think. She just mentioned in the faculty room about going to a parent teacher conference soon. I don't know how she juggles it all.'

My stomach bottomed out. If Erica wanted me to stay away from her and Brock, that was one thing. But she had a daughter that was the same age I'd been when Brock violated me. No, no way. Fuck school, or Brock's threats, or any of it. That little girl couldn't be under the same roof as him.

'I'm sorry, Mr. Walker, but do you mind if I pack up a bit early? I want to try to catch Erica.'

'Of course,' he glanced at his watch. 'She usually leaves about now, so you may want to hurry.'

I nodded, grabbed my bag, and hustled to her office. She wasn't there. So I ran to the parking lot outside her building and caught a glimpse of her walking in the distance. Thank goodness it was still light out, otherwise, I don't think I would have spotted her.

'Erica!' I called, and she stopped and turned. I ran and wove through the parked cars until I reached her.

'Lana,' she said tightly, though there was a look of sadness in her eyes.

'Listen, I know what you said about not wanting to hear my side about Brock, but you have to. You have a daughter. She's the same age I was when he raped me, and I don't care if you kick me out of school or tell the dean or any of it. You have to know. She's not safe under the same roof with him. Please, please, just listen to me and believe me—'

'Why?'

'Because you're a mother who I believe would do anything to protect her daughter,' I said. 'A few weeks ago, I wouldn't have been so certain that parents would do that, but now I know just how deep a parent's love can go. How deep it should go.'

I'd seen it with Bea. How she cared so much about Cal and Jack. How every day, in every decision they made, she worried for them. Loved them. Supported them.

Indecision played across Erica's face.

'Even if I am lying, don't you think your daughter is worth figuring out the truth?'

'Yes,' she whispered.

I stopped mid-rant. 'Yes?'

She nodded and glanced around. 'You're right. I'm sorry, Lana,' she said with the same quiet voice. 'Jamie, my daughter, never liked him. And I was just so happy to not be in this alone, to feel loved and like I had a partner that I didn't want to believe you.' She looked up at me, and what I saw there had my stomach hollowing out. 'But I do now.'

'Oh, God, did he hurt her?'

'No,' Erica said, and tears filled her eyes. 'No, he didn't, but I've realized some things about him recently, and I . . . he's not who I thought he was.'

She started to cry. I gripped her shoulders. 'Did he hurt you?'

'No, nothing like that. Just beneath the good-guy mask is someone I don't want near my family.' She shook her head. 'God, Lana, I'm so sorry. For everything.'

'It's okay.'

'No, it's not.'

'All I'm worried about now is you and Jamie. Can you get away from him?'

'I was going to tell him it's over tonight, and stay at my mother's for a while.'

I nodded. 'Don't be alone when you tell him. Have someone there, or do it over the phone, but don't let his temper come out when you're alone.'

'I know.' She pulled me in for a big hug and said one more time, 'I'm so sorry.'

I wanted to tell her it was okay. That she and her daughter were safe, and that's all that mattered. She didn't need to be sorry to me. But she just turned and got into her car and drove off. It was then I realized it was a silver 4x4.

The same car Cal described leaving my house after the break-in.

'Oh, God . . .'

Cal had been called out to a fire, so I had to wait until he got back to tell him what I'd discovered. In the meantime, I was done letting Brock mess with my life. It was clear Erica had the 'getaway car' from the night of the break in, which meant Brock was the one in my house. And he wanted something.

But what?

I opened my front door and walked in. Dropping my bag, I started looking through my desk, files, anything he might think could be valuable. I had no idea what he could possibly want. It was like searching for a mad man's treasure.

'What the hell are you after?' I said to myself, looking through my box of important documents. Just my birth certificate, insurance policy—

A booming knock came at my front door.

'Lana!'

It was Brock. And he sounded pissed. I took a deep breath and walked to the door. There was still some daylight left, and I was across the street from a fire station. I had my phone in hand, just in case. But it was time to confront the bastard.

'What do you want?' I asked, opening the front door.

He was almost red with fury. 'For starters, I'd like to know where my fiancé ran off to.'

I swallowed hard. 'How would I know?'

'Don't fuck with me. I know you said something to her, and now she's gone.'

'Good,' I said.

He growled and kicked the door the rest of the way open and stormed in. I backed up and fear flooded. I dialed 9-1-1, but before I hit send, he grabbed the phone and threw it across the room.

I was terrified. Those eyes, that rage . . . I knew it all too well, and it made the little girl inside want to scream and cry. No, I needed to stay calm. Stay focused. Try to rein in the fear and get out of this.

'Why were you here? I know it was you who broke in.'

He scoffed. 'You're so fucking stupid. You have no idea what you're dealing with.'

'I know I'm dealing with a sociopath in front of me, and you can't scare me anymore.'

'Oh no? You look pretty scared right now.'

He stepped closer, and I backed away until I hit a wall. 'Get out!'

He smiled like a devil would. Sinister and viscous.

'You keep sticking your nose where it doesn't belong and fucking with my life.' That was laughable. I fucked with his life?

'If fucking with your life means you can't get to Erica or Jamie, I'll gladly do it.' I found all the strength I had and forced the words, 'Now, get out.'

Rage took him over and he lunged at me, grabbing my throat and pushing me further against the wall.

'You fucking bitch. You won't take everything I have! You won't!'

I clawed at his arms and kicked out, making contact with his shin, enough for him to ease his grip. Instinct took over, and I kicked again, and again. He threw me against the desk, which tipped over and crashed. I caught my breath for a moment, and when I saw him coming at me, I knew by the look in his eyes he was going to kill me.

I kicked out again and hit his stomach, but he grabbed me as I tried to run, and wrestled me to the floor.

'Help!' I screamed. 'Help!'

Putting my hands together, I made a double fist, and just started hitting any part of him I could. Fighting. For the first time since that night, I fought. I fought the way I wanted to back then, but had been too afraid. Not today. If he wanted to hurt me, I'd hurt him back. And I would fight. For myself, for Erica and Jamie, for everyone who'd been hurt and couldn't fight.

'You can't beat me,' he said, and spit landed on my face. I struggled and used all my strength to get him off of me, and when I saw his hand raised high, I squeezed my eyes shut.

The next thing I felt was blistering pain slice across my cheek. He hit me so hard I blinked to clear the haze, but it wouldn't clear.

I hiked my knee up and kicked him hard, finally hitting his groin and getting him to scream in pain. He rolled off of me with his hands cupped between his legs. I made for the door, threw it open, and screamed.

'Help!' I ran toward the fire station. 'Help!'

A couple men ran from the building, and I breathed hard. 'He attacked me . . .' I sputtered and pointed at my house.

My ears were buzzing, I couldn't hear right, couldn't see right. But one man ran across the street to my house, while the other said something I couldn't make out.

But I felt a hand on me and flinched away.

'Easy, it's okay,' I thought he said. 'It's me, Dave.'

'Dave?'

He started yelling for a medic or gurney? I couldn't quite hear right, but I was glad he was a familiar face. My mouth was moving, but sounds didn't come out. I was trying to tell him what happened. Tell him that Brock was over at my house and to not let him get away. I struggled to stay standing, and felt like my limbs suddenly lost the bones in them.

Then a big fire truck rolled up and parked in the driveway.

Cal jumped from the truck in all his gear that was smoky and covered in soot and ran toward me.

Everything would be okay.

Just seeing him made me know that.

But my adrenaline crashed, and as I watched Cal run toward me, all I could hear were the words he once said the last time this happened.

When you crash, I'll be right here to catch you . . .

With that, my legs buckled, and my world went dark.

Chapter 22

My body was being jostled around, and I opened my eyes to find Cal staring down at me. I glanced around. There was an IV in my arm, something securing me around my middle, and a clip thing on my finger. A faint *beep, beep, beep* sounded, matching the pulse in my neck.

'Ambulance?' I asked.

Cal nodded. He stroked my hair and looked on the brink of a nervous breakdown. He didn't have his heavy fire jacket or helmet, but his red suspenders came up over his blue T-shirt, and he still had on his fire pants and boots. Flecks of ash lined his handsome face.

'Brock!' I said, and tried to sit up, but found it difficult because my neck was in some kind of wrap.

'Shhh, it's okay, Kitten. The police came and took him into custody.'

'He was looking for something. Said I was taking things from him.'

'It doesn't matter,' Cal said softly, and ran his fingers along my hairline. 'I don't want you to worry about that. I want you to rest.' He looked at Rhett, who sat across from me. 'What are you running?'

'Standard drip for hydration. Her BP is a little low, vitals are good, though.'

They were talking over me like I wasn't there. Cal looked so stern, tense, I wondered if this is how all people felt riding in an ambulance. Being my first time, I didn't know what to expect, other than it seemed like overkill for a dizzy spell.

'I don't need a hospital. I'm fine, I just collapsed.' I tried adjusting my shoulders, but it was no use. I was strapped down pretty well. The smell of rubbing alcohol tied with the sound of sloshing liquids as we hit a rough patch of road surrounded me.

'We're already en-route, and you're going to get checked out,' he said sternly. 'Can you tell me what happened? How he got in your home and where were you were hit?' He stared at me, and it looked like he was about ready to cry. 'Besides the face,' he said softly.

Yeah, I figured I must have a good welt on my cheek because it was throbbing like hell.

'He just pushed me some, the only big hit was to my cheek. I'm really okay.'

Cal scoffed, and ran his thumb along my non-bruised cheekbone. 'I'm sorry, Lana, I should have protected you better.'

'You did. You have. I went home, I opened the door to him. I just wanted to know what he was looking for, because it was him. The man that night was Brock.'

'How do you know?'

'Erica, my old advisor, she drives a silver 4x4, and I talked with her today.'

'She helped him?'

'I don't think she knew what he was planning. But she left him. I told her the truth and she believed me and left him today. He blames me, and that's why I think he was angry, but . . . '

There was more. Something was going on, and I didn't know enough to understand it. He said I was stupid, like things were going on in front of my face that were bigger than I could imagine.

My head just pounded.

'Don't stress about that, love,' Cal said. 'You're safe, and it sounds like Erica is away from Brock, and he's in jail for at least the night.'

We pulled up to the hospital and the doors opened to take me out on the bed. Cal was right beside me.

'I fought him off.'

Something proud and terrified and sad and happy marred his perfect features. 'Yeah, you did, love. I'm so proud of you.'

'No concussion,' the doctor said, as I sat in the hospital bed and he looked over my chart. I had been there a couple hours, they ran all the tests that Cal insisted on. 'Aside from a few bumps and bruises, you look to be in good shape.'

Bea was sitting next to me and squeezed my hand. Her quilted vest was over a long-sleeved sweater, and she smelled like sugar cookies. I knew it was her and not just her home. I wanted to snuggle against her and melt away from the sterile world of the hospital.

She was teary and just kept mumbling what sounded like thanks to God as she kept me close. It was foreign, but soothing at the same time. Having her there. Caring.

Cal was clutching his cell as he frowned at the doctor. 'You sure she's okay?'

He nodded. 'Yes. Just some rest and Tylenol for any discomfort. There is a small fracture in your cheekbone,' he said to me. 'It will heal on its own, but will be tender in the meantime. None of the blood vessels in your eye seem to look bad, but if you have a problem with vision or headaches, let me know.'

Cal scrubbed a hand over his face and looked like he was about ready to lose it.

'Hey,' I whispered to him. 'I'm okay.'

He just shook his head, and I was pretty sure he was about to smash his cell phone in his grip. Thankfully, it rang and he looked down, relief and anger lit his face.

He kissed my forehead. 'Hang on, I'll be right outside.' He put his cell to his ear and said, 'Hey, yeah . . .' and walked out of the room.

'He's just worried about you,' Bea said. I knew that. He was so worried it made him angry and upset with himself, which was what I didn't want.

'You're lucky, young lady,' the doctor said, and patted my shoulder.

'She's a fighter,' Bea said, as she put an arm around me and pulled me close. The doctor nodded and gave me a prescription for Tylenol with codeine to help me sleep. When he opened the door, I caught a glimpse of Cal in the hallway with fury on his face.

'He fractured her fucking cheekbone,' he said into the phone before the door closed again.

Bea just continued to hug me. 'He's probably just yelling at the officer who took Brock in.'

I took a deep breath. I appreciated Cal's concern so much, but I hated that he was internalizing it.

'None of this was his fault,' I said to Bea, and she nodded.

'I know, honey. But he feels out of control right now.'

Her words hit me. This was how Cal held his control. In every other area, he let me express what I needed, be who I was, even exercise my own dominance from time to time, but this? My safety and wellbeing were his personal mission, and he was spiraling. Just like the night I saw him scared when I took the sleeping pills.

Cal came back in and shoved his phone in his pocket. He looked at me, and I saw so much raw fear and dread on his face.

Seeing this big man in half his fire gear looking at me like I had some kind of power over him broke my heart. Because he was the one I needed. The one that came through for me.

'Baby?' I asked him softly. His gaze snapped to mine. 'Will you please take me home?'

'My home,' he said.

I nodded. 'Yes, take me there, with you?'

'Yeah,' he said, helping me up.

'I'll drop you two off,' Bea said, which was nice, since we'd arrived in an ambulance.

'Thank you,' I whispered.

Cal just cradled me into his side, and walked me out of the hospital like I was the most precious thing he'd ever held. And the thought made me want to cry for a whole new reason.

Chapter 23

Standing in Cal's bedroom, he lifted my shirt over my head slowly, then peeled my pants off. Though he was gentle, there was nothing sexual about his undressing me. He had a purpose.

'Do you still have to work tonight?'

'Talked to the captain, told him there was a family emergency. Got it covered. I'm not leaving you.'

He did only live a couple blocks away, but still, I didn't want to put him in a bad place with work.

'It's not really a family emergency. Will the captain be mad if—'

'You're my family, Lana,' he said, cutting me off. Those words struck my chest so hard it felt like thick syrup. Family. He'd made me part of his, and it was something I wanted so badly.

He unclasped my bra, slid it down my arms, then pulled a shirt from his dresser. But he stalled as he looked me over, his big hand gently smoothing over my shoulder, down my chest to my hips. He knelt and looked at my legs.

'You have a couple bruises,' he said, gently tracing over my shin bone.

'I was kicking pretty hard.' I smiled.

He didn't seem to like my humor, simply stood and walked behind me to inspect further.

'I'm really okay,' I said.

He came back around to face me and softly put the T-shirt over my head and pulled it down.

'Let's get you to bed.' He fluffed the pillows, then threw back the blankets and helped me in, tucking them in around me like I was a child.

'I'm just going to take a quick shower and hit the couch.'

'What?' I understood the shower, because the poor guy was still smoky from whatever fire he'd crawled out of earlier, but the couch? 'Why aren't you coming to bed with me?'

'I don't want to hurt you.'

'You won't. My cheek hurts a little, but I'll take the medicine.' But that wasn't the real reason. 'I want to feel you next to me.'

'No.' He turned and walked toward the bathroom, and I heard the water turn on. What the hell? Why was he pushing me away now?

I threw back the blankets and marched in after him. I didn't bother waiting, or even taking off the shirt he'd put me in, I just walked right into the shower with him.

'What the—' he spurted, wiping water from his eyes.

'Yeah, exactly,' I said. 'What the hell?' I stood there, the spray hitting me just enough to dampen the white T-shirt and mist my skin.

'Lana, go back to bed. I'll bring your pill, and then—'

'And then you'll "hit the couch?"' I shook my head. 'Why are you keeping me close and staying away at the same time?'

'Because I don't want to hurt you. I already told you that.'

'You won't.'

'I will,' he snapped. 'I love you, damn it. I'd never hurt you. In any way.' His eyes were wild with fear and so much pain I wanted to shake him and hug him at the same time. 'Look at you,' he said, glancing down the front of my shirt. My nipples were peeking out of the now-see-through cotton, and Cal definitely noticed. 'If I get too close to you, I'll want you in a way I shouldn't.'

201

'Baby, I want you too. You won't hurt me.'

'You're injured!' he snapped. 'You just fought off an attacker, your cheek is swollen, and I'm not going to risk hurting you further.'

'But, I need you,' I said. 'I want to feel you and I want our connection. I was so scared,' I admitted. 'No, I was terrified. I felt weak, and forced myself to be strong and fight. And I did. Now I feel good. I got away, Cal. I beat him this time. Now, I just want you to hold me. Make love to me. I don't want to be alone, I want to be with you.'

He shook his head and went to cup my face, then stopped and pulled back. 'I want to so much, love,' he said. 'But with how I'm feeling right now, it's not a good idea.'

'How are you feeling?' I asked.

He looked at me for a long time, as if debating on whether or not to tell me. Finally, with a scowl and a few more seconds, he said, 'I'm scared too.' He took a step closer, all wet skin and muscle, and my body screamed for him. I was desperate to feel him. I reached out and ran my palms along his abs. He closed his eyes for a moment, as if my touch soothed him. I hope it did.

'I was terrified too. When I saw you with blood on your face and you looked at me like I could save you. Help you. When I saw you fall, I barely got there to catch you.'

'But you caught me. And I fell because I was relieved. My brain shut down and I passed out, but I knew I was okay. You were there.'

'You made yourself okay. You kept yourself safe. But the realization of how close you came to—' it looked like he bit his tongue before continuing. 'It could have been worse. I could have lost you.'

'I'm right here. I'm reaching out for you.'

Such a difference from how we started our relationship. I was now the one seeking him out.

'And I want to reach back, but I'm so angry. I look at your face, at what he did to you, and I want to kill him. I want to rage and break shit. I want to bury myself inside you, not letting you even an inch from me.'

I glanced down and saw his muscles all flexing with tension and his cock hard.

'Please,' I whispered. 'I don't want to be an inch from you either.'

With a heavy frown, he turned off the water and peeled the shirt and my panties off and left them in the shower. Reaching for a towel, he gently dried my hair and body that had gotten damp.

Helping me from the shower, he quickly dried off and led me to the bedroom and laid me down like he had before.

'Under the covers,' he said.

I looked up at him, 'Only if you're coming with me.'

I held out my arms and waited, praying he'd stay.

Finally, he slowly sank down, and I parted my thighs to cradle him. He had all his weight on his arms.

'You won't hurt me,' I whispered, and brought him down for a kiss. I pulled the blankets around us, and he lowered himself to his forearms, then looked at me to gauge my reaction.

'I'm okay,' I assured him. I wrapped my legs around his hips, his cock nudging my entrance. 'This,' I reached down to grip him and rolled my hips enough to take the tip of his cock inside me, 'is where I want to be. You are what I need.'

He groaned and kissed me softly as he slowly pushed further inside.

Tension poured off of him like he was holding back from scooping me up and hugging me hard. But he didn't. He was so gentle, touching me like a butterfly's wings.

He pushed forward until he was buried to the hilt, and I exhaled in happiness. Connection. Him. What I needed.

He didn't retreat, just gently rocked, feeling me, kissing my face softly down to my neck. His rhythm didn't quicken, he just kept stirring, refusing to leave my body for an instant. He bent his head to kiss along my breast and gently pull a nipple between his lips.

I ran my hand through his hair, every sensation lit up my nerves, and all I felt was pleasure and bliss.

I was okay.

We were okay.

Everything in the world was righting itself.

He pumped deep, my orgasm coming on slow and intense. He kissed up my neck again to my mouth. Tasting his lips was like coming home. A home he made me feel a part of. Like family. The one thing I never truly had.

'Cal,' I whispered against his mouth. He looked at me, and I cupped his face. 'I love you.'

He frowned, like something struck his chest, but there was a sadness and happiness behind his eyes. I was hoping, in time, the sadness would go away and all that would be left was joy.

'I love you. So damn much,' he said, and kissed me harder this time. Staying deep, his chest pressing against my breasts and feeling his warm skin envelope mine, I gave myself over to the pleasure and came apart in his arms.

I felt him harden further and come right behind me. My name on his lips as he did. This was home, I was certain of it. Right there with Cal. The thought made me so happy and so relaxed, I couldn't help but close my eyes, and get lost in the warmth.

Chapter 24

I woke up and winced. The sting in my cheek was throbbing and ached. Cal's big body was pressed against mine, his arms tucked close to his chest, as if he feel asleep telling himself not to touch me.

I grinned a little. He was so worried, but a step had been taken, and he could see that I wasn't breakable. Despite the events of tonight, and the annoying ache in my cheek, I was feeling relatively good.

I glanced at the clock. It was two in the morning. I quietly got up and went into the kitchen where my prescription was and got a glass of water.

I read the front of the bottle when Cal's phone caught my eye. It was blinking.

When I went to tap a button to make it stop, a texted popped up. My heart stopped. It was from Jack.

Jack: How is she?

I gasped. Cal had told him what happened? I should put the phone down now. Bea told me that Jack's distance wouldn't have stopped them from being brothers. Sure, they must communicate now and again. As well they should. But about me?

Put. The. Phone. Down.

I bit my lip. Jack asked how I was . . .

I clicked the text and the conversation thread got brought up.

Nothing prepared me for what I started reading. My eyes went wide as I scrolled through their texts back and forth. Certain phrases sticking out to me like:

Jack: I thought you had this handled.

Cal: I do. She's stronger than you give her credit for.

Jack: I give her plenty of credit. Which is why I can't fucking stand this.

Cal: We agreed . . .

Jack: I know.

That was when Cal and I first started dating. After my run-in with Brock at my car at school several weeks ago.

We agreed?

What did that mean? I looked at the call log, and what I found was shocking. They spoke sporadically after Jack first left. But more recently, the back and forth was regular. More calls and texts had been exchanged in the last two weeks. It was Jack that Cal had been on the phone with at the hospital. He'd kept him up to date on me? On us?

'What the hell?' I whispered. When another text came through.

Jack: We need to talk. Now.

My thumb hovered over the keys. Pain and sickness were lining my stomach. I didn't know the extent of what was going on, but Cal and Jack had some sort of agreement.

I typed back: What is it?

I waited a heartbeat, and Jack came back.

Jack: What is it? Lana got fucking hurt tonight. This changes everything. And this goes deeper than we thought.
Something bad has happened. I'm calling this off early.
You've had your time.

I frowned. What goes deeper? Brock's hatred for me? This code they're speaking in?
You've had your time . . .
My heart beat faster as I scrolled through the texts, going as fast as I could back to when Jack left. Finally, I found the date.

Jack: It's done. She's yours.

My vision wavered, and I realized it wasn't because I'd been hit, it was because tears were lining my eyes.

'Lana?' Cal asked, standing in the entrance of the living room and looking at me. I held his phone and turned to face him. He looked at it, then at me.

'Jack is trying to get ahold of you,' I whispered.

Horror crossed his face.

'In fact, it seems like you and Jack have had a plan from the beginning.'

'It's not what it looks like,' Cal said, and took a step toward me.

I bit my bottom lip to try to keep from crying. My eyes already hurt with the strain. 'Really? Because it looks like you two made arrangements to share me.'

'Love . . . listen to me—'

'It's done, she's yours?' I asked, glancing at his phone. 'You've had your time?' God, all of it came together. Jack had said our timing was off before he left. It even looked like part of him wanted to stay. But he didn't. Because it was Cal's turn to have me?

I couldn't hold back the tears anymore. The moments from the past flashed through my mind. The night I met Cal. The night at the bar I met Jack. The day they spoke outside the bar and I never saw Cal again until after Jack left.

'You set me up. Both of you did.' The tears that escaped hit my cheek and stung. But nothing compared to the last half of my heart breaking. 'You've had your time?' I repeated one of the messages again. 'Tell me you didn't pass me between the two of you like some toy. Tell me you didn't have an agreement to share me.'

I waited, and he said nothing. My entire chest burst open. Nothing compared to this kind of blow. I thought Brock was bad? Thought Jack leaving hurt? This was unfathomable pain, and it sliced straight through my sternum like shears.

'Tell me!' I yelled, and tossed his phone on the counter.

'We both wanted you,' he said softly. 'The first night at the bar, we both saw you and wanted you. But when the fight broke out—'

'You took care of the fight that was happening at my table, and Jack took care of me.'

'I let you two be,' he said. 'But when I saw you show up to the barbeque, that wasn't planned. Jack had left town, I thought maybe it didn't work out, and I still wanted you.'

'Well, lucky me.' Tears were streaming faster as I looked at the man I trusted. The man I thought would be in my corner, and the whole time he was cavorting with the man that *was* my corner. 'What about the bar? The talk outside?'

'We were both shocked. The timing was off. He was gone, then I was gone to a wildfire . . . '

'What did you discuss outside?'

It was the one thing Jack never told me. The one time when everything shifted.

'Jack made his claim, I backed off.'

'No!' I said and tears came faster. 'Tell me all of it.'

Cal closed his eyes for a moment. 'After he left . . . we came to an understanding. We both wanted you, so it seemed like our only option was to . . . '

His stare held mine, and so much anger and hurt rose.

'Say it,' I demanded between gritted teeth.

'Share,' he whispered. He stepped closer. 'But not like it sounds. I was crazy about you from the start, but in the end I agreed to back off because of Jack. But after you two broke up . . . '

'You were right there to swoop in.'

'He knew I wanted you. I told him and I was honest about everything. He was gone. And I wanted a shot to prove to you the man I could be.'

'Then what?' I cried. 'How was this grand plan supposed to end?'

Cal paused. Whatever he was about to say was clearly painful. Eventually he forced out the words. 'Jack still has feelings for you.'

I froze. I felt those words like a punch to my gut. I would have given anything to hear those words just a few short weeks ago. Now I felt as though my world was falling apart. How could everything have changed so much, so incredibly quickly? And if Jack still cared and Cal *knew*, then why . . . ?

As if he heard my unspoken question, Cal continued, 'He

stayed away so I could have my time, just like I respected his time. Then, you could decide.'

'Decide what? Who broke my heart more? Who destroyed my trust better?'

'No, decide who you wanted back.'

I scoffed and shook my head. 'All this time, you lied to my face.'

'I was trying to give us a chance. Trying to give you and Jack a chance. Everything got messed up after that meeting between him and your dad and Brock.' He shook his head. 'We were going to tell you.'

'That doesn't make it better, Cal!' My breath was catching, and the world wouldn't hold still. 'Everything you said, the both of you said, was a lie.'

'No, it's not. I love you. Jack loves you. We never lied about that.'

'He left! People who love don't leave.'

'Jack – he has his own issues. He had to go, he needed time,' Cal admitted. 'And then after we . . . then I wanted him to stay gone, so I could have time. With you.'

'So you two held to your agreement? How noble.'

'Lana, please,' he took another step.

'Don't. Don't you dare,' I said. I walked past him into the bedroom and pulled on my pants and jacket.

'What are you doing?' Cal asked.

'I'm leaving,' I said.

'No.'

'You don't get to tell me what to do,' I said, and put on my boots and walked back to the kitchen, grabbing my prescription.

'We never meant to hurt you. We tried to give you a choice.'

'And what if Jack and I never broke up? Then what?'

Something heavy in Cal's eyes pierced my stomach. 'I wouldn't have interfered. And I would have spent the rest of my life wondering.'

'Well, you don't have to wonder anymore. I gave you everything I had left to give,' I sobbed. 'And you broke it.' I wiped the back of my hand over my eyes and winced from the pain of my cheek and the pain of my world crashing down.

Something like water looked to line Cal's eyes.

'Please, love, don't go,' he begged, a sharp edge catching in his voice. 'Remember when I held you, I asked you to remember that moment. Remember that even when things get hard . . . remember that moment.'

'The one where you promised you'd always be on my side? That you'd always chase after me? That you'd fight for me and with me?'

He nodded.

Tears streamed down my face. 'That moment doesn't matter anymore.' I looked him in the eyes. 'Because your promises mean nothing. You've already won. You got me to feel for you. Got me to move away from Jack and toward you. I don't want you to chase me anymore.'

'But, I love you.'

'People who love also don't lie,' I whispered.

His phone buzzed, it was Jack calling.

I glanced at it, then at him. 'You better get that.'

With that, I walked out the door.

Chapter 25

I ran as fast as I could. It was the middle of the night, but my house was only a couple blocks away. Cal would have to at least put on pants first before he could catch up to me, so I had a head start. That is, if he did chase me. Which I was hoping he wouldn't. Because, no matter how hard I ran, how loud my body screamed in pain, I couldn't stop.

I heard sirens and lights flash from the fire station just a block ahead. They were going out on a call? Only the truck didn't go far, just pulled into the middle of the street.

I slowed and saw smoke.

'No . . .' I raced faster. The smoke was coming from my house. 'No!'

I ran up and my little yellow house was in flames, burning as if soaked with gasoline and glowing in the night.

Everything I'd ever owned, ever valued, was in there.

'Whoa, stay back,' Dave caught me.

'It's my house.'

'Is there anyone in there?'

'No.' Thank God, Harper was out of town. She was safe. I bawled and watched as my entire life, literally, went up in flames. 'What . . . how?' were the only words I could get out.

Dave clearly didn't have time to explain, but did say, 'The fire went up quick, we can tell by the flames and how fast it's burning already that some kind of lighter fluid was used.' With that, he ran toward the truck.

Oh, my God. Someone *set* my house on fire? If fluid was used, this was no accident.

'Lana!' Cal yelled, and ran up next to me.

I pushed away from him and walked to other side of the street. I wanted to scream and cry. The pain was so real it felt like it'd taken up residence in my entire body and would soon topple me over.

'Lana, listen to me,' Cal said, cupping my shoulders. 'You're in trouble.'

I shook my head. I was so overwhelmed with everything. 'Why would Brock do this? Why?' I looked at Cal. 'Why would *you* do the things you do?' Everything was crumbling.

'That's just it. Brock's in jail. They're holding him overnight. He couldn't have done this.'

That meant Brock wasn't alone, and whatever they, he, whoever, wanted from me was big, or they wanted me dead.

My mind went blank like a curtain of shock overtook it and forced me to stop thinking. Too much. This was all too much.

I sat on the curb across the street from my burning house and held my head in my hands. The sounds of men yelling, tires screeching, and the fire roaming all rang in my ears like a bad dream.

'Lana,' a deep voice that I recognized called out. I knew that voice. I knew it so well it sent shivers up my spine. I looked up to find Jack. He resembled some kind of dark knight in his black coat and pants. His eyes were as onyx as the night that surrounded us, while an orange glow from my house haloed him.

I couldn't move. Couldn't speak. I wanted to yell at him. To curse him and tell both him and Cal right where they could jump off. But I sat there, dazed and destroyed, with every ounce of my will, my world, burning and crumbling like my home.

'Baby,' Jack rasped, and knelt to face me. The endearment hit something in my soul that made me want to hate him even more than I loved him. 'Whatever plans you have of pushing Cal and me away are going to have to wait,' he said, as if he could read my mind. 'You're in danger. Do you understand?'

I just looked at him.

Snap.

I just snapped.

'Are you kidding me? I haven't seen you in months!' I shot to my feet, and Jack followed suit. He was flanked by Cal, and they both stared at me, their towering frames hovering. But I would have none of it. 'You lied to me! Left me. Messed with my life and my emotions and . . . ' I gripped my head. 'My house is burning! And you stand here and tell me what I'm going to feel and what I'm going to do?'

'Yes. Because you are our first concern,' Jack said.

'You don't get to make me your concern. Either of you. You both lost that right when you lied to me, made me love you, then broke my heart.'

'Lana, this is serious. Love, something bad has happened. Your—'

'I know! I'm staring at it!' I pointed at my house.

'No,' Jack said sharply, his dominant voice snapping me to attention. His eyes softened and he stepped toward me. 'Baby,' he whispered, 'I'm so sorry, but your father is dead.'

NOT the end . . .

Look for *Yours Forever*, the third
and final book in the Reign Series.

Book 1 in the Reign Series,
Yours Tonight, is available in
all good bookstores and
ereaders everywhere!

For more books by Joya Ryan,
visit her site www.JoyaRyan.com

Acknowledgments

Thank you Anna, Grace, and the amazing team for all your hard work on this book. Thank you Jill Marsal for being the best agent in the galaxy. Thank you E-book formatting fairies for the wonderful edits. Thank you to my incredible family and friends for supporting me.